ADRIFT

C. G. COOPER

"ADRIFT"

Book 1 of the Daniel Briggs Novels

GET A FREE COPY OF THE CORPS JUSTICE PREQUEL SHORT STORY, *GOD-SPEED*, JUST FOR SUBSCRIBING AT CG-COOPER.COM

Warning: This story is intended for mature audiences and contains profanity and violence.

DEDICATIONS

To our amazing troops serving all over the world, thank you for your bravery and service.

Semper Fidelis

CHAPTER ONE

Y*our fault*. The accusation floated along the edges of my subconscious, teasing me, blaming me, haunting me. I moved to swat the thought away, but my hand smacked into something hard. Wincing, I tried to open my eyes. They felt caked closed, rebelling from the night before.

The smell of must and dirt made their way into my muted senses. Finally cracking my lids open, I saw that I was lying on my side, facing a hay bale. I tried to rise, my stomach lurching at the movement. I closed my eyes again, willing the nausea to subside even as the spike headache stabbed painfully. Where was I?

After a few deep breaths, I eased to my feet, clutching a moldy wood railing for support. Tongue scraping along my parched lips, I looked around, squinting at the bright rays of sunshine streaming in through a crack near the door.

"He's around here somewhere," came the shout from the sunlit morning.

"Let's check in the barn."

I ducked behind two stacked hay bales just as three figures stepped into the barn, cautiously peering into the relative darkness. As my vision adjusted, I saw that one of the guys, a hulking figure in overalls, had a bandage covering his nose, the next one, almost a twin to his buddy, had his arm wrapped in a sling. The others looking healthy, one sporting a baseball bat, the other a long crowbar. By their appearance, they looked like brothers, or at least cousins.

"You two look behind the hay, I'll take a look up in the loft," Mr. Busted Nose whispered harshly.

They'd find me in a second, and I didn't want to hide.

"You guys looking for me?" I asked innocently, standing up, stretching with a yawn.

Their eyes whipped around at the sound of my voice. "You've got some payback coming, boy," said the leader.

"I'm sure we can talk about this, fellas. Why don't..." I started as the farmboys cut off my lanes of retreat.

"Ain't gonna be that easy. You broke my nose and busted Honey's shoulder. There's..."

"Wait, his name is *Honey*?"

Honey's face turned beet red. "Let me take him, Johnny. I swear he's..."

"I told you he's mine," said Johnny, slowly pulling an old revolver out of his pocket. "Now, it's up to you whether you just lose your pecker or I fucking kill you."

I raised my hands, not wanting a fight, wondering if my weakened body would respond to commands. "I don't want any trouble, why don't I just walk away before we do something stupid."

"You shoulda thought of that last night, faggot. Tell you what, I'll give you a chance. You take my cousins and win, then *maybe* I'll let you walk away."

I looked over at his cousins, noticing the bulbous nose of one and the cauliflower ears of the other. They were fighters. "Let me guess, boxer and wrestler?"

The cousins both smiled wickedly, showing off their yellowed teeth. Surprising they still had them all.

"Doesn't seem fair to me," I said. "I'd be happy to pay for..."

Without warning, the boxer cousin charged, swinging his baseball bat, aimed straight at my pounding head. Click.

My mind switched and reflexes took over. Crouching under the lumbering swing, my fist smashed into his groin, his momentum taking him over my right shoulder. *One down.*

Cousin #2 roared, but came on more tentatively, sobered by the easy takedown of #1. *Thwap. Thunk, thwap*, came the swings, hitting the elevated hay bales and railing, narrowly missing my dodging body. He was methodical, slowly corralling me into a corner.

The chop came, and I stepped into it, catching his hands overhead, a dribble of tobacco juice seeping out of his grimacing mouth. We struggled there for a moment, knowing that in a straight up strength contest, #2 would win. Not a possibility. I stepped wide with my left foot, swung my right leg behind him, and kicked back, pulled forward with my arms, flipping him over my right hip.

He landed with a thud, barely stunned, but I was on top. *Take out the threat*, came the order. #2 looked up, eyes wide, seeing the demon in my eyes, hand cocked, ready to deliver the death blow.

"I think that's enough," came a deep voice, followed by the rack of a shotgun shell.

I didn't lift my eyes, still poised to strike, seething.

"Let him go, son," came the order from whoever had entered the fray.

It took an extended moment. Inside, I uncoiled, easing off my opponent.

"Now look here, Mr. Herndon, this guy attacked us..."

"Let me guess. This happened at Pappy's last night?"

"Yes, sir. Sent me to the hospital with a broken nose, and Honey with a bum shoulder."

"Seems like I already heard the story, Johnny. A little bird told me you boys were harassing that pretty little waitress and this kid stepped in. Now, you gonna tell me that didn't happen?"

Johnny hesitated.

"That's what I thought. Why don't you take your cousins on out of here. Enough fun for one day."

"But Mr...."

"I said, get your tails off my property. I could just as easily call the sheriff for trespassing and assault. Your choice."

The leader of the redneck band grumbled, but ended up gathering the wounded and headed out the barn door.

CHAPTER TWO

I waited until I heard the rumble of an oversized muffler, and the gravelly spin of large tires on the dirt road to come out from behind the hay bales.

"You okay, son?"

"Yes, sir. Thank you, sir."

The old man, sporting a slight potbelly, cradled his shotgun now pointed at the ground. "I don't mean to sound inhospitable, but I think it's time for you to hit the road."

"Yes, sir. I'm sorry for trespassing. Would it be okay if I paid for my stay?" I slid a fifty dollar bill out of the tightly packed wad in my back pocket.

The old man cocked his head, taking me in. "Where are you headed, son?"

I shrugged. "Just passing through. Didn't mean to cause trouble."

"Well, you did get into it with the wrong family. Those boys, the Laneys, their grandpa owns half the county. I'll just say that Johnny and the boys get most what they want. Tell you what, how about you come inside and I'll get you some coffee and breakfast, maybe even a shower," he said, pointing at my dirt-stained clothing.

"I don't want to get you in any trouble, sir. Maybe it'd be best if..."

"Now, I'm not afraid of them boys, but the choice is yours. The road's that way, and the house is that way. Take your pick. I hope to see you in a minute."

My unintended host left, and I stood there staring at the open door. I'd hurt so many, I didn't want to take the chance of this kind old man paying for my sins.

I stepped around the hay bales, grabbed my ruck sack, and headed for the door.

————

THE SMELL of bacon and coffee pulled me as I knocked on the wooden frame of the rickety screen door.

"It's open," came the call from inside.

I eased the door open with a *screeek*, taking off my well-worn boots and leaving them on the porch. Following the sounds of metal clanking and scraping against metal, I found the old man in front of a gas stove, scrambling eggs while tending to the quarter inch thick bacon in a skillet.

Part of me salivated, but another part churned.

"Hungry?"

"I think I will be, sir."

He looked up from his cooking, wrinkles squinting appraisingly. "Why don't you take a quick shower? Bathroom's just around the corner. I put some old clothes out for you. You can throw yours in the washer when you're done."

I nodded, not knowing what to say. He pointed an impatient finger down the hallway. "I'm not gonna ask again son, you stink. By the time you get done, I'll have breakfast waiting."

I smiled, the first I'd allowed myself in days.

———

AFTER CHUGGING what felt like a gallon of water out of the faucet, I stepped into the steaming shower, grateful for its soothing caress. Not wanting to keep my host waiting, I washed and rinsed quickly.

The clothes he'd laid out were slightly big for my shrinking frame, but a roll on each sleeve and pant leg made them more than wearable.

By the time I walked back into the kitchen my stomach was grumbling. The old man looked up as I walked in. "Feel better?"

"Yes, sir. Thank you." I took a seat, my mouth watering at the sight of the greasy plate in front of me.

"You mind if I say Grace?"

I shook my head. The old man bowed his head. "Lord, thank you for this bounty, and thank you for the fellowship of our new friend..."

I squinted through closed eyes. He was waiting. "Daniel, sir. Daniel Briggs."

He smiled warmly, closing his eyes once more. "Thank you for the fellowship of our new friend Daniel. May this day be filled with joy. In Your Name we pray, Amen."

"Amen," I mumbled, more as a thanks to the old man's kindness, than for any spiritual reverence.

I watched as he made a sandwich between two slices of toasted white bread with his eggs and bacon, focused like a child. He looked up with a mouthful of breakfast sandwich, as if coming to a realization. Swallowing the bite whole, he said, "How rude of me. Hollister Herndon at your service, Mr. Briggs. My friends call me Hollie."

I nodded, refocusing on my meal. Hollie took the hint

and dove into his sandwich, which reminded me of my past. I used to make sandwiches out of everything. Faster to eat that way. Better when you were on the run.

————

HOLLIE GAVE me a quick tour of the farm before setting out to check the fields. "Damn deer been eating everything this year," he grumbled. I offered to go along, but he suggested I rest. "You still look a little green." He was right. My hangover raged into Round 2, so while Hollie rode the fields, I gladly dozed in a leather armchair, grateful for the cold air inside, warding off the stifling summer heat outside.

I was careful not to fall completely asleep. Deep sleep brought thoughts, feelings I didn't want. So I dozed, occasionally sipping on a large glass of iced water that sat next to me on an antique side table.

————

"WHAT DO you mean he's still there?"

"I told you Johnny, old Hollie let the guy into his house. Hasn't left yet."

Johnny Laney gripped his cell phone angrily. Old Man Herndon had always had a streak of rebel in him. Johnny's grandfather had lived with an uneasy truce brokered years ago with Hollister Herndon. Stepping foot onto Hollie's land went against his grandfather's orders.

"You just keep an eye on him. I want to know when he leaves."

Johnny would have his revenge, even if it meant bending his family's laws. The blonde stranger would pay.

————

HOLLIE RETURNED AT NOON, sweat stained and flushed. "It's a hot one out there." He poured himself a glass of sweet tea and gulped it down in one shot. "Now that hit the spot."

"Any luck with the deer?" I asked.

"Nah. Saw a couple, but they were too far out. They're getting smarter every year. Bolder too. Never used to come out during the day."

"Can I ask you a stupid question?"

Hollie turned, pouring himself another glass of tea. "What's that?"

I was embarrassed to ask. The question alone would tell him something wasn't right. "What town is this?"

He looked at me for a moment, putting the pieces together in his head. "This is Defuniak Springs, Florida. Just north of the Gulf of Mexico. How'd you end up here if you don't even know where here is?"

"Got on a bus in North Carolina, had a few drinks along the way. From what I remember, we stopped. I guess it was here in Defuniak Springs, I hit the bar next door to the gas station, and the rest you know. I guess the bus left without me."

Hollie put the pitcher of iced tea back in the fridge, took another sip and looked at me. "You running from something, Daniel?"

I didn't know how to answer the question. This man was a stranger, a kind stranger, but still a stranger. "If you mean, am I running from the law, no."

Hollie studied me. I knew he wanted more, but in the end he didn't press. "How about we head over to the barn and load up some hay?"

————

THIRTY MINUTES LATER, after loading ten bales into the back

of Hollie's old pickup, and driving down a single lane dirt road running the border of his and a neighbor's land, we reached our destination.

"You can just throw them out there," pointing to the side of the road. I looked around, wondering why we were unloading in the middle of a field, when I heard a tinkling, followed by a handful of cows emerging from a copse of trees. I hopped out of the cab and into the bed of the truck, easily tossing the bales over the side. By the time I'd thrown the last bale out, the cows were hungrily tearing into the tightly packed meal.

I jumped down and climbed back into the cab. Hollie slowly turned the truck around, careful to avoid the distracted cattle. We headed back the way we came.

"Are those your cows?" I asked.

"Nah. Belong to my neighbor. Nice old lady. Lost her husband a few years back. I do what I can to help. She used to have a couple hundred head of cattle. Now what you see is what she's got."

There were no more than ten or twelve cattle in the small herd. "What happened?"

Hollie shrugged. "Max Laney took it all."

CHAPTER THREE

Johnny Laney paced back and forth. He'd been summoned by his grandfather, who was keeping him waiting in the grand foyer of his largest home.

"Come in here, Johnny."

Reflexively, Johnny took off the ball cap he'd been wearing. He walked deeper into the house, entering the spacious living area with floor to ceiling windows overlooking the pool and grotto.

"Jesus, boy. What the hell happened to your nose?"

Johnny reached up and touched his nose tenderly. "Got in a little bit of a scuffle is all, granddad. No big deal."

"That's not what your uncle said. He tells me that Len and Randy came home busted up this morning."

Johnny shuffled uncomfortably.

"What are you not telling me?"

"It was nothing. We were just horsin' around."

"What about last night? Were you going to tell me about the fight at Pappy's?"

Johnny's eyes looked up in shock. "How did..."

"How did I find out?" Maximillian Laney stood up from

his chair, looking every bit the patriarch he was, gray hair slicked back, Tommy Bahama shirt untucked over khaki pants and suede loafers. "You think there's anything that happens in this town that I don't know about?"

"No...no, sir."

"You're goddamn right!" Max Laney calmed as quickly as he'd risen to anger. "Now, tell me what happened last night."

———

HOLLIE LET me make dinner that night. I grilled the inch-and-a-half thick rib-eyes while he made up corn biscuits in the same skillet he'd used for the bacon. That, along with canned tomatoes from a roadside vendor, made it the most enjoyable meal I'd had in ages. We ate silently, savoring the marbled steaks as they melted in our mouths.

A shot sounded from far away, probably at least two miles. My ears perked up and I looked to the window. Hollie kept eating. "That's just the neighbors. Probably shooting at coyotes."

"You have a lot of them around here?"

"Just like the deer, they seem to be making a comeback. Laws changed a while back, made it illegal to hunt them. Numbers swelled. Now they say we can kill them again."

"Why do you shoot them?"

"They get into everything. Had a friend lose close to fifty chickens in one night. Another lost half a dozen calves to a pack of coyotes. In fact, I've been meaning to take a few out myself, just haven't had the time. What do you say we head out after dinner and see if we can't bag us a few?"

I nodded silently, eyes on my plate.

"You do know how to shoot, don't you?" he asked.

"Yes, sir."

"Now, let's not go back to this *Sir* business. You don't have to come with me, but I sure could use an extra set of eyes. Mine aren't what they used to be. If you don't want to shoot, you can spot for me."

Every fiber in my body wanted to say no, but instead, I said, "Okay."

———

DARKNESS FELL as we setup in the second story silo above the barn. Hollie brought two shooting mats for us to lay on, along with a night vision scope and his Garand 30.06 rifle. I asked him about the beautifully maintained weapon.

"Got it as a gift after I came home from Korea." He didn't explain further and I didn't pry. It seemed that Hollie had his secrets too.

"How does it shoot?" I asked.

"Well, I've never put a scope on it, want to keep it like in the old days, but even without the scope I can get a decent grouping at five hundred yards."

"Not bad."

"You know anything about guns?" he asked.

I nodded.

We gazed out into the fading light, stars beginning to twinkle overhead. I took a slow breath, feeling the familiar anticipation.

———

WE DIDN'T HAVE to wait long for the coyotes. They slinked their way into the rows of corn that stood waist high, taking their time, almost like window shopping. "Five dollars says they're heading to Mrs. Nettle's chicken coop," whispered Hollie. "Probably looking for groundhogs."

Hollie settled behind the sights of the Garand, nuzzling

it, an old friend. "I can't see a damn thing. Must be my eyes. Here, see if you can. I'll spot for you."

Reluctantly, I took the weapon, checking the safety, eight rounds inserted with the World War II era 'en bloc' clip. Running a hand along the smooth wood stock, I settled back onto the mat, breathing slowed, my old rhythm, eyes over the iron sights.

"Can you see 'em?" asked Hollie.

"Yes."

"You ever fire a Garand? It's got a little more kick than what your generation is used to. Just sayin'."

"I'm okay," I said, simply.

My focus narrowed, tunnel vision encompassing the small portion of field, like an internal spotlight highlighting the target area.

"Fire whenever you're ready, son." Hollie watched expectantly through his night vision scope.

Breath in. Slow breath out. *BOOM*. Shift. *BOOM*. Shift. *BOOM*. Shift. Coyotes scattering. *BOOM*. Shift. *BOOM*. Coyotes bolting for the woods. *BOOM, BOOM, BOOM*. Eight rounds. Eight kills. The clink of metal as the clip ejected from the rifle, flying into the air, falling to the ground. Silence.

Hollie turned his head slowly my way as I checked the rifle's chamber out of habit, placing the weapon back in my host's hands. I rose, suddenly exhausted. "I thought you said you knew *a little* about guns."

I shrugged, climbing onto the ladder leading down to the ground.

"Hold on. That was some shooting. Eight hits at almost two hundreds yards, near dark." He stood up, I could see the look on his face. I didn't want it. "Where'd you learn to shoot like that, son?"

I looked up, struggling to hold back the emotion in my voice. "Marines."

Lowering myself to the ground, I went looking for my ruck sack, and the bottle of whiskey whispering to me in the dark.

CHAPTER FOUR

Snake Eyes! Snake Eyes! The call screamed in my head, desperate, pleading, dying.

"Daniel?!" a more muffled call came. "Where are you, son?"

Hay rustled as I shifted around. I was in the barn again. The last I remembered was taking a walk in the fields with my bottle of whiskey, trying to forget.

My bowels clenched as I struggled to stand, holding my stomach. "I'm in here, Hollie," I called.

A moment later, the barn door opened and Hollie entered, once again shotgun peeking through first. "Daniel?"

"Right here."

"What are you doing in here?"

I shrugged, making my way into the daylight.

Hollie looked at me, wanting to ask questions, instead, after a pause saying, "I've got some breakfast cooking. You come over when you're ready."

I watched him walk toward the house, me struggling to have the courage to face him. My bowels answered for me, and I hustled to the house, making a B-line for the bathroom.

———

THIS TIME it was country ham and eggs over-easy. Hollie waited patiently, saying Grace after I'd taken a seat. We ate without talking, him probably wondering whether I should go, me wondering the same.

We finished, tag-teaming the dishes, still without a word. Hollie dried his hands and said, "Follow me. I want to show you something."

Here it was. My out. "Hollie, I..."

"We can talk later, just follow me."

I nodded, walking behind him as he took the steps to the second floor. Pictures scattered along the hallway gave me glimpses of how Hollie used to be. Young and strong, working the fields, married.

Turning a corner, we entered a small bedroom. Hollie opened the closet, pointing to an old foot locker with HERNDON stenciled in white on the top. "Can you lift that up onto the bed?"

I picked it up, laying the wooden box softly on the comforter.

Hollie opened the foot locker, slowly, reverently. He picked up a black and white photograph and handed it to me. It perfectly captured the youth and exuberance of a young Army Lieutenant and a pretty girl. "That's me and Patty, right before I got shipped off to Korea."

"You were a Ranger?"

Hollie nodded, looking down into the container, lifting out another picture. It was in color, a young man, face painted in olive and black, floppy boonie cover, M16-A2 cradled, a wide white smile. "That was my son. Ranger too. Lost him in '92."

I understood. My father hadn't been a Marine, but plenty of my fellow Marines had followed in their family's footsteps.

We sat down on the edge of the bed, Hollie flipping through photos from his time as a Ranger. "This one was right after a night raid when we destroyed the 12th North Korean division headquarters. Dicey night, but we took it to 'em."

The pictures of destruction, craters, and bodies, threw my thoughts to my time overseas, another country, another time. I listened politely as he told me his stories, obviously struggling at times. I could tell that he hadn't shown his memories to many. Most of us didn't.

"How did you end up here?" I asked once he'd replaced the album.

"Dad died while I was in Korea. As soon as I came back stateside, I finished out my commitment and took over the farm. Momma couldn't run it by herself, in fact, the Laney family was trying to buy it from her, for a steal, of course. Dad hadn't left much money. I dug in, got us out of debt, and I've been here ever since."

Before I could ask another question, a horn honked out front. Hollie stood and pulled the lace fringed curtains aside. "Speak of the devil. It's Max Laney."

CHAPTER FIVE

"You stay here. I'll take care of him," Hollie said, already headed to the door. "Don't come outside."

———

"What can I do for you, Max?"

Max Laney, standing in the shade of the porch, wiping his brow with a monogrammed handkerchief, motioned to his grandson who waited near the Lexus SUV.

"I heard you're harboring a fugitive, Hollie. Doesn't sound like you."

"I don't know what you're talking about. I have a friend staying with me, but he's no fugitive."

Laney shook his head sadly. "That's not what I heard. Look at my grandson, got busted up pretty good the other night. Says it was your guest who did it."

"I don't know anything about that. Did Johnny tell you he was trespassing with three of his cousins yesterday morning, threatening me and my houseguest?"

Laney's eyes narrowed, and he threw a glare at his grand-son, who cowered slightly.

"Oh, he didn't tell you about that? Maybe I should be calling the cops?"

Laney raised his hands. "Now, Hollie, there's no need for that. Sounds like a couple kids having a toss. I seem to remember us doing the same thing a few years back."

Hollie grinned. "You never could take me, even with your posse."

Laney shrugged, no longer concerned. "I suggest you tell your *guest* to get out of Defuniak as soon as he can. Don't know what might happen if he gets caught in town. It's out of my hands."

———

I HEARD THE ENTIRE CONVERSATION, surprised that Hollie lied for me. He didn't have to do that. Why trust me?

A moment later, the Laneys left in a trail of dust. I heard the front door close, and went to meet Hollie at the stairs.

"You hear all that?" he asked.

"I did."

"I can't stand that son-of-a-bitch." Hollie shook his head, then changed the subject. "I've got some work to do. You okay to help me out?"

———

"LET me come back tonight and drag him out of the house, granddad. I can take care of it."

Max Laney kept his focus on the road, scheming as he drove. He'd wanted control of the Herndon land for over thirty years. Every other property surrounding Hollie's three hundred acres belonged to Max Laney in one way or another. Maybe he could use the situation as leverage...

"You won't do a damn thing until I tell you to, you hear me?"

Johnny nodded, smiling. It was the first time his grandfather had mentioned taking action. He could wait. Knowing his grandfather, it wouldn't be long.

———

WE SPENT the day touring the fields, taking soil samples, measuring moisture, inspecting the irrigation ditches. Hollie's land was fed by a decent sized lake and several underground springs. "It's why Laney wants it so bad. I'm one of the only self-sustaining plots of land in the area. He controls the water everywhere else. It's how he got his hands on the others. Control the water, control the land."

"How does he get away with it?" I asked, a complete novice to farming and land.

"It's all just enough within the law. Of course, no one would ever say Max Laney applied any extra pressure. He's an upstanding businessman, a man of the people. Doesn't ask for much publicly, but if you want anything done in Defuniak Springs, you'd better believe Laney knows about it, and, more than likely, gets a piece of the pie."

It sounded like the old west or the mafia to me. Maybe I was naive in the ways of modern business, but I couldn't believe it could happen in the current age.

———

JOHNNY PULLED into Pappy's Honkey Tonk gravel parking lot, next to four late model vehicles, taking the handicap spot. Chugging the last gulp of the Budweiser, he crumpled the can, threw it on the ground and opened the door to the bar.

It was smoky inside despite only two patrons sitting on stools, hunched over their drinks. A fat man behind the bar looked up at the sound of the door opening.

"Hey, Johnny. What can I get for ya?"

"Kelly in?"

The owner hesitated, assessing Johnny's mood.

"She's in the back."

"Get me a shot of Jack and a Bud, then go get her."

The owner put down the dish towel and moved to fill the order, Johnny taking a seat in the middle of the bar, keeping his gaze on the obese bartender.

"You know, you really should lose some weight, Wally," Johnny jabbed. One of the other patrons snickered.

The owner's face colored, but he chuckled nervously. "I know, I know. The wife's been telling me that for years." He set the shot glass in front of Johnny who took it and drank it, slamming the tiny glass down. "I, uh, maybe I should get back into the gym. Remember those days? You and me on the football field?" He handed the beer bottle to Johnny, hand shaking slightly.

"That was a long time ago, Wally. What'd you play anyway? Towel boy?" Another snicker from the drunk patron.

"Nah, hell. I was on the O-line with you, remember?"

Johnny nodded, sipping his beer. "Why don't you go get Kelly?"

A minute later, a skinny girl with sun-streaked hair, jean shorts hugging her slight form, walked in from the kitchen. "Hey, Johnny," she said tentatively, avoiding his eyes and the bandage on his nose.

"I need to have a word with you out back," Johnny said, pointing his bottle at the young girl who looked no more than twenty years old.

"Uh, I've got prep work to do in the kitchen. Let me ask..."

"Don't worry about Wally." Johnny smiled. "It'll just take a minute."

Kelly looked around for support. Wally had stayed in the kitchen. The customers pretended not to listen. She was all alone.

"O—kay."

Johnny pounded the rest of the beer and tossed the bottle behind the bar. "Next round's on me, fellas," he said to the others, one who looked asleep, but grinned at the offer.

Johnny led the way and opened the back door for Kelly, patting her rear as she passed. She knew better than to flinch.

CHAPTER SIX

After helping Hollie dispose of the dead coyotes and various random farm chores, I showered and headed to the kitchen for dinner.

Fried chicken, greasy and steaming, sat waiting expectantly. "Dig in," said Hollie, still tending the stove. "I've got collards coming too."

I didn't wait, starved. I'd polished off two succulent thighs before Hollie sat down, bringing the ham hock seasoned collard greens with him. As before, we closed our eyes for a quick blessing.

"You know, I really should be paying you for helping me out," Hollie remarked, taking his first bite of chicken.

"I think I'm the one who owes you. How about we call it even?"

Hollie nodded, not saying anything while we devoured a good portion of the food. "How long are you planning on staying? I mean, I'm not saying you have to leave, just curious."

I'd been thinking the same thing. It wasn't fair taking

advantage of his hospitality. "Not long. I've got some places to visit."

"Home?"

I shrugged, not wanting to think about visiting family. That could wait, despite my mother's pleas. She wanted me home. I wanted to be anywhere but.

"Do you think it would be okay if I borrowed your truck after dinner? I wanted to drive over to the bar and apologize."

"Sure, but you think that's a good idea? Might run into the Laneys again."

"I'll take my chances to make things right. Can you give me directions?"

————

AFTER HELPING WITH THE DISHES, I climbed into Hollie's pickup and headed out to the main drag. It took me just under ten minutes to get there. There weren't many cars in the lot as I pulled in, taking a moment to do a quick appraisal of the area.

Nothing looked familiar when I stepped into the bar. I must've been really drunk that first night. The bar stools were nearly full, but only one of the twenty odd tables held customers. No one looked up as I approached.

"Excuse me, is the owner in?" I said to the girl behind the counter, who was turned away from the bar, grabbing a handful of beers.

She swiveled around carefully, somehow holding six beer bottles in her tiny hands. Her eyes met mine, and she startled, almost dropping everything. "It's...it's you," she said, almost in a whisper averting her eyes, one of which I noticed was ringed in red and purple. A new injury.

"I'm sorry, have we met?" I asked.

Before she could answer, someone called out from the kitchen, "Kelly, get on back here and pick up this food."

She looked at me furtively, purposefully trying to hide her black eye with her streaked hair. "I'll tell Wally you're here."

I nodded and took a seat.

———

"WHY DIDN'T YOU FOLLOW HIM?"

"You told me to stay put, Johnny."

Johnny fumed. His idiot cousin didn't know how to take a shit without permission.

"You sure it was him?"

"Yeah. Blonde hair. Same guy."

"Which way did he go?"

"Headed towards highway ninety."

Johnny pictured the roadways in his mind, ruling out destinations. "Was Hollie with him?"

"No."

"There aren't many places he could've gone. Call me if he comes back."

Johnny put his truck in reverse, squealing out of the drive.

———

A MAN EMERGED from the back, wearing a grease-stained white apron. He scanned the dimly lit bar, his eyes finally settling on me. They went wide.

"You shouldn't be here," he said.

"I don't mean any trouble. I just wanted to stop by and apologize for the other night and see if there was any damage I could pay for."

The owner looked at me, deciding which way to take it. On one hand, I was offering him money, something a bar owner never said no to. On the other, he was probably risking the wrath of the town's thugs.

He pointed to the opposite end of the building where a jukebox pumped out an old Johnny Cash hit. I followed him over.

"You seem like a good kid, kinda drunk the other night, but you stuck up for Kelly..."

I put up a hand. "I'm sorry. I don't mean to interrupt, but my memory's a little hazy. Can you tell me exactly what happened?"

He looked shocked, but only for a moment. "Didn't think you were that drunk." He shook his head. "It went down like this: Johnny Laney was in his usual seat," he pointed to a table near the bar. "He'd been drinking most of the afternoon. You came in at some point, don't remember exactly when, sat at the bar and ordered a drink. Whisky, right?"

I nodded.

"Anyway, a little time goes by and Johnny and his cousin start getting loud, singing along with the music. No big deal. Happens all the time. Well, Kelly brings them a new pitcher of beer, and Johnny accidentally knocks it off the table. Kelly knows better than to piss him off, so she goes to grab a mop to clean it up. Johnny gets mad. Wants another beer right then. Kelly tells him she had to clean it or someone will slip. He doesn't care. That's what she told me. I was behind the bar."

A faint trace of recognition. Nothing concrete, just a shadow of a memory.

He continued, "Once Kelly got them more beer and finished cleaning up the mess, things went back to normal. That was, until Johnny asks Kelly to sit in his lap. She's a pretty little thing, I get it, but she's a good girl. She says no. Johnny didn't like that. He grabs her by the backside and puts her on his leg. Somehow she gets away, Johnny and his cousin laugh as she makes it back to the bar. I tell her I'll take care of their orders for the rest of the night.

"A couple minutes later, Johnny yells for more beer. I take them another pitcher and he asks where Kelly is. I tell him she's busy tending the bar. He doesn't listen. Johnny gets up, marches over to the bar, and points his finger in Kelly's face, telling her she better get over there and serve them. She was scared. I try to calm him down, but he's pissed. That's when you stepped in."

I felt my blood rising as he continued the story.

"You tell Johnny to leave her alone. He doesn't like that one bit. Walks over and stands right in your face. You don't move. The whole place is watching Johnny stare you down, screaming at you. You're like a statue, looked right back in his eyes. Then you say, I'll never forget this, "Are you finished?" It was like you put a red hot poker in his backside. He loses it, shoving his head right into yours, pushing you back over the bar. I grab the phone, ready to call the cops, but don't get there. You push him back and jackhammer him with your forehead. I see his nose squash, and Johnny goes straight down to the floor."

"And his cousin?" I asked.

"He comes over to try and help. You were calm as Sunday. He swings, you somehow grab his arm, twist, and pop that thing out of socket. He screamed like a little girl."

No wonder the Laneys were after me. I'd invaded their turf, disturbed their chokehold.

"Was there any damage, anything I can pay for?"

By the look on the owner's face, I could tell there hadn't been, but he was trying to decide whether to pretend that there had. Finally, he shook his head. "No. No damage, just some spilled beer."

I pulled out my dwindling stash and peeled off two one hundred dollar bills. He looked at them expectantly, probably salivating. "One last thing. What happened to her eye?" I asked, pointing at the waitress.

The owner hesitated. Telling a story was one thing. Getting involved was another. He looked at the money in my upraised hand. "It was Johnny. He stopped by earlier."

CHAPTER SEVEN

Johnny slammed his palm on the steering wheel. He hadn't found the stranger at the grocery store or the gas station. There weren't many places he could go. Johnny figured the guy probably wasn't out for a casual dinner. The only other place they had in common was Pappy's. Johnny made an illegal U-turn and headed that way.

———

I TRIED to talk with the waitress before leaving, but she did her best to ignore me. In the end, I ordered a soda, took a sip, and left a hundred dollar tip, hoping the owner would be smart enough to leave it for the girl.

It was time to move on. I'd already made enough of a mess in Defuniak Springs. I stood up from the bar stool and headed for the door.

———

JOHNNY SMILED as he pulled into Pappy's parking lot, instantly recognizing Hollie's old truck. "I've got him now."

————

I WAS ALWAYS CAREFUL, especially in unfamiliar places. It was the only reason the swinging bat narrowly missed my head as I exited the building, falling to the side to avoid the blow. My assailant cursed and moved to follow my roll. Looking up, I saw that it was Johnny Laney. I was in no mood for a fight.

"I thought we'd made our peace," I said, crouched and ready to dodge again.

Johnny's nostrils flared. "The only peace you're gonna have is when I dump your ass in the swamp."

Another swing, another dodge. He wasn't stupid and had apparently learned his lesson, careful to stay out of arms reach, instead using the length of the bat to keep me moving.

"I don't want any more trouble. I'm leaving..."

Just then the loud BLIP of a police siren, followed by its flashing lights stopped us both.

"Put the bat down, Johnny," came the call over the loudspeaker.

Johnny stood breathing hard, ignoring the order.

I heard car doors opening, and saw two policemen meandering over, guns still holstered.

"Come on, Johnny. I said, put the bat down."

By the sound of the cop's voice, it was obvious that he'd made the command because of his job, not because he actually wanted the bat lowered. *Are all these guys related?*

"This is none of your concern, Mitch," said Johnny, still focused on me.

"The hell if it ain't. You know I can't just let you beat some guy to pieces in public, Johnny. Now come on, put it down."

Johnny finally relented, lowering the weapon, but didn't drop it. He pointed a finger at me.

"He assaulted me first."

"Is this true, sir?" asked the cop.

"No," I said, still watching Johnny.

"Bullshit! How do you think I got my nose busted? Ask Wally. Ask Kelly."

The two cops looked at each other, making a decision. "Sir," speaking to me, "If we can please have you come with us, we'll see if we can't get this resolved."

"What do you want me to do?" I asked, concerned, not scared.

"Let's have you take a seat in the back of our squad car. We'll go in Pappy's and get some answers."

"Gentlemen, if you're going to arrest me I suggest you do it," I said, taking a gamble that the local cops might not want to go through the hassle of taking me in without a valid charge.

Another silent moment. Thinking. "Okay. Why don't we all go in there and ask Wally. If it's not true, we'll let you go. If it is..."

He let the threat hang. I could've run, hit the tree line, make a break. They didn't know who I was. I knew how to survive off the land, escape and evade. But something told me to stay, to see what happened. Maybe I was just curious about what the witnesses would say.

"Okay. Let's go."

———

JOHNNY LED the way back into the bar, me next, the two cops bringing up the rear. I saw Kelly flinch as we stepped in, quickly scooting back to the kitchen.

"Wally!" Johnny called.

The owner's head popped out from under the bar, a frown at our appearance. "How can I help you, officers?" he asked, trying to force a smile. Two of a bar owner's least favorite things had just stepped into his establishment: brawlers and cops.

One of the police officers stepped forward. "Mr. Laney said you and Ms. Kelly were witnesses to an assault on his person by this man," pointing at me. "Is that true?"

Wally was in a tough spot. I almost sympathized for him... almost. "Well, I'm not sure..."

"Tell him what happened, Wally. This guy broke my nose!"

Wally shuffled uncomfortably, wringing his hands on the filthy dish cloth he held. "Now, I'm not sure if I saw anything." His face changed, brightened. "But, you know, I'm pretty sure Kelly saw everything. Why don't I go get her?"

The cops and Johnny didn't protest. Wally had found his way out. The lie burned in my chest, something I would not forget.

Kelly stepped out a moment later, Wally forgoing any further questioning by hiding in the kitchen.

The officer asking the questions smiled at the young waitress. "Ms. Kelly, we won't take much of your time, but we wanted to get a statement from you regarding the alleged assault on Mr. Laney by this gentleman here."

Patrons tried to pretend not to listen as Kelly struggled to stay standing. Her petite frame shook under the white hot glare of Johnny Laney. She looked to me and I nodded, mouthing, *It's okay*.

Tears came to her eyes.

"Ms. Kelly," the policeman pressed, "will you kindly tell us what happened?"

Kelly looked at me again, unsure. I nodded again, not wanting her to take any more heat from the bully standing next to me. Suddenly, she stood a little straighter and said, "It was just a little scuffle, officer. I didn't get to see the whole thing, but I think it was a misunderstanding."

Johnny seethed. The policeman exhaled. "Are you telling me that you *did not* see this man break Mr. Laney's nose?"

Kelly looked right at Johnny, her hair parting just enough to show her black eye, roughly concealed by makeup. I knew the cops had seen it too. "It all happened so fast. Like I said, it was some kind of disagreement. I don't think I'm the best witness."

"You lying little, bitch," growled Johnny. The number two cop put a hand on Johnny's shoulder that he promptly shook off.

"Calm down, Johnny. I'm sure Kelly wouldn't lie."

They were trying to diffuse the situation, correctly putting the pieces together in their heads. They knew where Kelly's black eye had come from. She wasn't Johnny's first victim, but they didn't want to open that can of worms.

The lead policeman turned to me. "You're free to go, sir. I would recommend staying away. It might be for your own good."

"Yes, sir." I nodded at Kelly, who resisted the urge to nod back.

"Come on, Johnny. Why don't I buy you a drink?" offered Cop #1.

The two on-duty policemen ushered Johnny to the bar, patrons making room. I could feel the younger Laney's glare on the back of my head as I walked out the door.

CHAPTER EIGHT

Hollie was on the front porch, whittling a piece of birch when I got back.

"Everything okay?" he asked.

"No damage."

"That's good. No trouble either?"

I shook my head. "Nothing I couldn't handle." He turned his gaze as I sat in the white rocking chair next to him.

"You sure?"

I nodded. "What do you know about the girl that works at Pappy's? Kelly?"

Hollie grunted. "Kelly Waters. Nice girl. Her daddy used to own a farm a couple miles down the road. Had to sell it. Now he works at the beach, taking care of vacation homes for out of town owners."

"What about her? Has she always worked at the bar?"

"I don't know. Don't spend much time there myself. Gave up drinking a fews years back. Why do you ask?"

"Just curious."

Hollie wanted me to say more, knew there was more, but

didn't press. Instead, we sat back, enjoying the cooler air, the smell of a storm coming.

———

THE TWO COPS, who happened to be distant relatives of the Laneys, stayed for a couple rounds then hopped back in their police cruiser and continued patrolling.

Johnny stayed, taking drink after drink, eyes focused on the muted television showing highlights of the day's games. Not a word came out of his mouth, just the repeated double thump of his empty glass on the bar.

Kelly kept pouring and Johnny kept drinking.

———

MEN DOWN. Men down. Insurgents overrunning....

I WOKE with a scream stifled in my throat, sweat soaking the sheets. Same dream. I hadn't had a drop of alcohol. My medicine. I couldn't go back.

As quietly as I could on the creaking wooden floors, I padded to the bathroom and rinsed my face off. There was a knock at the door, "Everything okay, son?"

I opened the door, the vanity light illuminating Hollie's concerned face.

"I'm fine."

"I heard screaming. Thought it was the coyotes for a second."

"Sorry. Didn't mean to scare you."

"Need anything?" he asked, still not prying, just worried.

"I'm okay. I might go for a little walk. Clear my head."

———

I HAD breakfast ready when Hollie came downstairs just after sunrise. "Now *that* smells good. Whatcha got in the oven?"

"Just an old recipe my mom taught me. I hope you don't mind that I used the rest of your eggs and most of your sausage. I can pick some up later."

Hollie waved the thought away, peeking into the hot oven. "I get all my eggs from a neighbor. Have a friend that gets me all the sausage I want too."

He set the table as I pulled out the casserole, setting it carefully on a hot pad in the middle of the kitchen table.

"I'm thinking that I'll probably head out this afternoon. There's a bus coming through at two o'clock," I said while we ate.

Hollie slowed his chewing. "You got your mind made up?"

"Yes, sir. I think it's best for everyone if I move along." I'd thought about it all morning. Kelly, the girl at the bar, Hollie, they'd be in trouble because of me. I couldn't add that to my already burdened conscience.

"You mind helping me with a couple things before you go?"

———

TOM AND MARY FREEMAN spent at least one week every year at the beach. It was their favorite place in the world, and if they'd had more money, they would've visited more often.

As they'd done every morning since arriving, the Freemans walked along the sandy shore, admiring the emerald water beside their beloved Rosemary Beach community. Mary carried a mesh bag full of shells. She'd add it to their collection at home.

"What's that up ahead?" Tom asked, pointing.

Mary squinted. "Something big. Maybe it's a dead dolphin. Let's go back. I can't stand to see the poor things like that, and besides, the last one we saw stunk to high heaven."

"You stay here. I'll go take a look."

Mary sat down on the snowy sand, burying her feet as her husband moved further down the beach. The form was half-buried, so he couldn't tell what it was. *A sea turtle?*

A seagull swooped down and landed on the form, picking. It looked up as Tom approached, holding something in its beak. *What is that?* he thought, now twenty feet from the prostrate form covered in sand and seaweed. The seagull squawked, causing it to drop whatever had been in its mouth, then flew away. Tom looked down. *Is that...*

A frothy waved crashed against the shore, jostling the form in the sand and moving aside a portion of the seaweed. Tom fell back horrified, tripping over his feet, trying to get away.

"Mary, call 9-1-1!"

CHAPTER NINE

Wally busied himself in the bar, picking up trash before sweeping and mopping the floor. He'd left Kelly to close up the night before. Normally she was good about leaving the place spotless. Hell, she was his best employee.

He'd returned in the morning only to find the place as he'd left it, dirty and sticky. After opening the doors to air out the stale smell, he pulled out his phone and called Kelly. It went to voicemail. He tried again. Voicemail.

"Hey, it's Wally. Just want to see why you didn't clean up last night. I'll take care of it for you this time, but let's not have it happen again."

He was upset, but he knew the value of a dependable employee. There were a few over the years, Kelly being one of the best.

Wally got back to the task at hand, dumping the last batch of plastic cups in the trashcan before he started on the floors.

"Yes, ma'am. When was the last time you saw her?" asked the police dispatcher.

"I think it was before she went to work yesterday," said Mrs. Waters.

"Is there anyone she could be staying with? Maybe a boyfriend or girlfriend?"

"Kelly doesn't have a boyfriend. She comes home from work the same time every night. I'm so worried. What can you do?"

"Technically it hasn't been twenty-four hours, but I'll let the chief know. I'm sure he'll have the patrols start looking."

THE WALTON COUNTY SHERIFF'S DEPARTMENT had cordoned off the beach, lining the perimeter with deputies and vehicles.

"Did you get any ID off of the body?" Sheriff Karl Tasker asked one of his men who'd just inspected the deceased.

"No, sir."

"What about cause of death? Any clue?"

"No gunshots as far as I could see. The coroner should be here any minute."

The affluent beach community hadn't seen a dead body in quite some time. Three local mayors had contacted the sheriff, asking if the cause of death had been determined and whether a suspect was in custody. He'd told them all the same thing, that the matter was still in its infancy, and that he would give them an update when he could.

Word spread quickly, and the crowds showed up before the police could get the body covered. Pictures of the body had already been posted on social media. Karl Tasker, a former beat cop from Detroit, fumed at the thought of having the poor girl's family see the photos. He wanted to wring the necks of the inconsiderate bastard who'd done it.

Tasker's phone rang. "Tasker."

"Karl, it's Darryl up in Defuniak Springs," Tasker rolled his eyes. He hated dealing with the chief of the Defuniak Springs police department. The man thought he was God's gift to law enforcement, when in fact, all he was just a lazy bigot.

"How can I help you, Mr. Knox?"

"Word on the street is that you've got a dead body on the beach."

Tasker waited for the question. None came. "And??"

"Well, it's still premature, but we got a call a few minutes ago. Seems that we may have a missing person."

"And you think..."

"Yeah, I know it's a long shot, but I was wondering if you could tell me if the deceased is a young girl, around twenty years old."

Tasker froze. "Can you send me a picture?"

"Sure. Want me to text it to you?"

"That would be best. I'm at the scene."

"I'll have one of my people send it. You should have it in a minute."

Two minutes later, the picture came through. It looked like a high school photo. The girl in the image was cute, not pretty. She smiled shyly at the camera, her green eyes squinting slightly.

"Mike, come take a look at this."

———

JOHNNY WOKE TO A SPLITTING HEADACHE, sun shining down on his face. He looked around groggily, realizing that he was in the bed of his truck. He could hear cars driving by. Pushing himself up with his arms, he peered out of the truck. *Not Defuniak Springs.*

It looked like 30A, or as tourists called it, SoWal, the beaches of South Walton. As he rose to climb out and drive home, something fell out of his lap. A pink cell phone.

————

"Knox, it's Tasker."

"What'd you find out, sheriff?"

"I've got some bad news."

————

"Daniel, I've gotta run to the store. How about you keep at it? I'll be back soon."

I nodded and turned back to the twelve-by-twelve shed we'd framed. Hollie was good with his hands. I was too, just not in traditional ways like carpentry. Still, I enjoyed the labor. It allowed my mind to focus and stay engaged. *I could get used to the farm life*, part of me thought. But I knew it wouldn't work. There was a timeline to keep. In a few hours, I'd be on my way.

Putting the thought out of my mind, I got back to cutting the lumber to Hollie's specifications.

————

"Mornin', Hollie," greeted the woman at the grocery store. "Anything I can help you find?"

"No, ma'am. Just pickin' up some odds and ends. How's Horace?"

The woman rolled her eyes. "He's still milkin' that back

injury. Just wish he'd get around to fencin' my garden. Them deer love my tomatoes."

Hollie moved along, picking up a plastic shopping basket. "You tell him that I said to get up off his old Air Force rear and get to work."

The woman chuckled, returning her gaze to the magazine she'd been reading.

He moved up and down the narrow aisles swiftly, thinking about how he could get Daniel to stay. It wasn't just the help, for which he was grateful, but he liked the young man. He wanted Daniel to have a place to stay, and Hollie wanted to give it to him. It'd been too long since he'd had company. Besides, there was something Daniel wasn't telling him. It was there, just beneath the surface.

Hollie wouldn't pry, but he'd known plenty of military vets over the years. He knew the toll they paid. If his new friend was in pain, he wanted to help.

Once everything on his list was packed into the basket, Hollie headed to the register. A customer and two cashiers were all looking up at the TV mounted on the wall outside the manager's office. News. No one turned as he placed his things on the conveyer belt.

"What's going on?" The words had just left his lips when a picture flashed up on the screen. It was a photo of Kelly Waters.

CHAPTER TEN

I was almost done with the cutting when Hollie pulled in. He unloaded the three grocery bags wordlessly, and walked into the house to put them away. *Strange. Not even a hello.*

I kept at it until every piece of wood was stacked neatly, waiting for further instruction. Hollie didn't come out, so I went inside. He was in the kitchen, staring out the window.

"Everything okay, Hollie?"

He almost jumped, turning around to face me. "I'm fine... I...I need to ask you something, Daniel." The lines in his face seemed deeper, darker.

"Sure."

"I'll just come right out and ask...where did you go on your walk this morning?"

I was confused. It was a strange question.

"I took a walk through the fields. Sat down for a while. Waited for the sun to come up."

Hollie nodded sadly. His demeanor frightened me.

"What's wrong, Hollie? What am I missing?"

It took him a moment to respond. He looked up, a strange look in his eyes. "Kelly Waters is dead."

———

JOHNNY PULLED INTO THE GARAGE, longing for his bed. Hopefully his grandfather was out. He was not in the mood to talk.

Creeping through the house, he sighed as he reached for the knob of his bedroom door.

"Where the hell have you been?" asked Max Laney from down the hall.

"I was out."

"With whom?"

"Who cares?"

"I care! Now tell me, where were you last night?"

"Come on, granddad, can we talk about this later? I'm beat."

The elder Laney sneered. "You'll sleep when I tell you to sleep."

Johnny exhaled, smelling his stale breath. His bowels rumbled. "I was at Pappy's."

Max's eyes narrowed. "Where did you go after that?"

"I fell asleep."

"Where?"

"In the back of my truck."

"At Pappy's?"

"No, down the road."

The patriarch searched his grandson's face, probing for the lie. "Have you seen the news?"

"No, why?"

Max Laney growled, "Come with me."

Johny reluctantly turned away from his door and followed his grandfather.

Breaking News

Police have confirmed that the body discovered in Rosemary Beach was that of local resident, and Walton High School graduate, Kelly Waters. Local law enforcement are asking for assistance in finding information pertaining to what is now being called an accidental drowning. If you have information, please contact the Walton County Sheriff's office at...

———

"You wanna tell me you had nothing to do with that?" asked Max Laney.

Johnny's stomach turned. Images in his mind. "I...I'm not..."

"Dammit, Johnny, this is serious. If you want my help, you need to tell me right now or you're on your own."

Sweat broke out on Johnny's back as patchy memories flooded back. The next thing he knew, he was telling his grandfather everything he could remember.

———

"What do you mean she's dead?" I asked, picturing the girl's face, the way she'd stood up to the cops and Johnny Laney the night before.

"They found her body washed up on the beach this morning. A couple of tourists found her."

"But, who would..."

"Daniel, you need to tell me everything that happened at the bar last night."

I lowered my head and told him.

CHAPTER ELEVEN

M ax Laney padded over to the kitchen table and picked up his buzzing cell phone.

"Max speaking."

"Mr. Laney, it's Darryl Knox. I was wondering if I could talk to you for a minute."

"Anything for our chief of police."

Knox paused.

"You still there, chief?"

"Uh, yes, sir. Well, it's just that it's sort of a sticky situation, and, well, I don't wanna come across wrong."

Laney mouth pursed, but he answered brotherly. "Come on, Darryl, we go back a long way. Why don't you just come out and say it? I won't bite."

Another pause.

"I appreciate that, Mr. Laney." Laney heard the police chief shift the phone. When his voice came again it was hushed. "I assume you've heard about the Waters girl?"

"I have. Damn shame."

"Well, we've begun the investigation, and we had the

chance to question a couple witnesses. One of them says that the last person to see her was your grandson."

"Which one?"

"Johnny, sir."

"Well that's quite a charge, son. May I ask who your witness is?"

"It's still an ongoing investigation, and I can't talk about the identity of any of our witnesses."

"I understand that, Darryl, but if you'd like my help, which I'm assuming you do, I'm gonna need a little more than what you're giving me. The last thing I want to do is call up my lawyer. Is that what I should do?"

Knox was in a tough spot. Sure he was the chief of police in Defuniak Springs, but Max Laney was the de facto benefactor of the community. Knox had played ball with Max's oldest son, Johnny's father. It was Max Laney who'd suggested to a young Darryl Knox that he put himself in the running for chief of police, despite his youth. The help of the Laney family name had solidified his promotion against strong opposition and the nomination of a former police chief from Brooklyn.

"Now, I don't think it's that bad, Mr. Laney, but I sure would like to talk to Johnny."

"How about I bring him down to the station and the three of us can have a little chat? Would that help?"

"I'd really appreciate that."

"Fantastic. We'll see you later this afternoon."

Maximillian Laney ended the call and closed his eyes.

———

HOLLIE WAS quiet as I finished the story, turning his folded whittling knife absentmindedly in his hand.

"I'll pack my things and go," I said, turning to leave.

Hollie snapped out of his trance.

"Now why in the hell would you do that?"

"I'm sorry?"

"Why are you running away? Seems to me that you've been doing a lot of that recently."

My fist clenched involuntarily. "What's that supposed to mean?" My temper rising.

"All I'm saying, is that if you're just another dumb grunt, pack your things and leave." He stared at me, hard. "But I don't think that's you. I think you're smart. I think you were trying to protect that girl."

The tension went out of me. All of a sudden I felt so tired, helpless. "What does that matter now? I got her killed."

Hollie's voice rose. "Wait just one goddamn minute. Who on earth said that it was your fault, because I sure as hell didn't?"

His words surprised me. The kind man who'd allowed me, a stranger, to stay on faith alone, was suddenly replaced by a person who reminded me of my lead drill instructor at Parris Island.

"What can I do? Who's going to take my word over the Laneys'?"

Hollie slammed his hand on the table. "I'll tell you what you won't be doing. You won't be feeling sorry for yourself in my house. Now are you a Marine or aren't you?"

I looked up at him, a smile forming, and said, "Always."

———

"TAKE a shower and put some decent clothes on," Max Laney commanded his grandson after barging in and waking him from a dead sleep. Johnny knew better than to refuse.

"Where are we going?" Johnny dared to ask.

"I'll tell you in the car. Now hurry up, we've got some things to talk about."

———

Wally was sweeping off the concrete slab by the front door when an SUV pulled into the lot. It was still early for customers. Wally shaded his eyes from the sun to see who it was. His stomach went to his throat.

Max Laney and his grandson stepped out of the vehicle and walked his way.

"Afternoon, Wally. You got a minute to talk?" asked the elder Laney.

"Y...yes, sir."

CHAPTER TWELVE

Hollie paced the room as I took in his new persona. He was all business. "Now, I'd put my money on Johnny, but I doubt there's a soul who would testify against him."

"Is their family that connected?"

Hollie laughed. "Max Laney not only owns half the land in this town, he also owns most of the officials."

"How is that possible?"

"It started years ago. He's bankrolled political campaigns and pressured officials to get *his* people in office."

"What about the police? Can he really manipulate an investigation?"

"He won't do it overtly, but I'm sure he'll throw his weight around in subtle ways. Without evidence or witnesses there's not much the law can do to convict someone."

I shook my head in disbelief. "We've got to do something."

"If the law doesn't, we will. I say we do a little digging and then wait and see what the police come up with."

It was too passive for my taste, but I deferred to Hollie's judgement. He knew the personalities in town.

We laid out a plan, playing out scenarios which all turned out to be wrong.

———

"MR. LANEY, THANK YOU FOR COMING," Police Chief Darryl Knox shook his guest's hand reverently.

"Like I said over the phone, I thought we could sit down and get to the bottom of this mess. Johnny's agreed to tell you everything he knows."

Johnny stood a respectful distance behind his grandfather, his head bowed. "Yes, sir. I want to help in any way I can. I still can't believe..." Johnny sniffled, wiping his nose with the back of his hand. "I'll tell you anything you want to know."

Chief Knox nodded sadly and led the way to the conference room.

———

I SCANNED the road while Hollie manned the wheel. It was a short drive, and familiar. We pulled into Pappy's parking lot and Hollie drove to the opposite side of the building.

"Just in case," he said as he put the truck in park.

We headed toward the back door. It swung open before we got there.

"Oh, I'm sorry, Hollie," the owner said in surprise. He had a bag of trash in one hand. His eyes widened when he noticed me. "You!"

"Now, Wally. We just want to have a word," soothed Hollie.

Wally dropped the bag and stepped back. That was when I noticed the blood running from his scalp.

"Are you okay?" I asked, pointing to his head.

He reached his hand up and came away with a finger covered in blood. "I'm fine. Just a little bump."

"It doesn't look fine. How about we come inside and I'll take a look at that."

Wally hesitated, his eyes never leaving mine, as if I were some kind of monster. "I don't want *him* coming anywhere near me," he said, pointing at me.

"Is that any way to treat a customer? Come on, fellas. Why don't we head inside out of this heat? I don't know about you but I sure could use a glass of iced tea."

Hollie ignored the proprietor's look and walked past him into the bar. I followed and a moment later, so did the portly owner.

The place was a wreck. Half the tables were either broken or overturned. Most of the liquor bottles lie broken beneath the far wall like someone had used them for target practice.

"What happened in here?" Hollie asked.

"Nothing I can't fix. I don't mean to be rude, but I've got some cleaning up to do. What was it you wanted to talk about?"

"Why don't you go fetch a wet towel and some ice so I can take a look at your head. We'll talk then."

Wally nodded and scooted around the corner of the bar, searching for a clean towel.

"What do you think happened?" I asked, in a voice only Hollie could hear.

"I think we're not the only ones who paid Wally a visit. By the looks of his head, it was pretty recent. We may have gotten lucky with our timing."

Nothing about the situation felt lucky. In fact, a nagging feeling told me that we were ten steps behind. Whoever had wrecked the place was after something.

Wally returned with a bag of crushed ice and a stained towel.

"Sit down right here and I'll take a look."

The bloodied owner flopped down, suddenly looking in pain. He winced at Hollie's probing. "Damn that hurts."

"It got you good. You might need stitches. Want us to give you a ride to the hospital?"

Wally shook his head vehemently. "I'll be fine."

Hollie looked at him for a moment and continued to clean the wound, finally wrapping the plastic bag in the bloodied towel. "Make sure you keep pressure on it."

The bar owner nodded. "What did you want to talk to me about?" he asked, ready to have us leave.

"I wanted to ask about Kelly Waters."

Wally's shoulders slumped. "Poor girl. Best waitress I ever had."

"What happened after I left last night?" I asked, not wanting to stick around any longer than needed.

"Why do you care? Isn't it the cops' job to ask questions?" he replied indignantly.

"Was it the cops that did this?" I pointed to the mess all around us. "Doesn't seem like something they'd do."

His bravado disappeared as quickly as it had come. "It's gonna cost a lot to get this place back together." He was lost in his own misery.

"When was the last time you saw Kelly? Did she leave with somebody?" asked Hollie.

"I...I can't say. I mean..." Tears flowed as Wally struggled to maintain his composure.

Hollie put a comforting hand on the man's shoulder. "We're not here to make trouble. We just want to get to the bottom of what happened."

"But I can't. They told me..."

"Who is they?"

"I can't tell. They'll kill me."

Hollie looked at me. Dread filled my gut. It felt like the night before when Kelly had stood up for me. I didn't want this man to do the same. He'd pretty much confirmed what I'd thought.

"It's okay. You don't need to tell us. Believe me when I say that the last thing I want is for you to get hurt." I started for the door.

"But…" Hollie started.

"It's okay, Hollie. We'll figure it out some other way. Sorry about your place." I reached into my pocket and pulled out three crisp hundred dollars bills, setting them on the bar. "This isn't much, but I hope it'll help."

Hollie followed my lead, and we headed to the door. As I opened it, hot summer air blanketing me in an instant. I turned suddenly. "Did Johnny stay after the cops left last night?"

I could see the inner struggle as Wally deciding how much to say. In the end he didn't say a thing, instead he nodded.

I did the same, and walked out the door.

———

"WELL THAT SURE IS SOME STORY." Sweat beaded on Chief's Knox's forehead as he made some final notes. "Anything else you'd like to add?"

Johnny sat across the conference table, never making eye contact. Max Laney sat stoically next to the police chief, his gaze never leaving his grandson.

"No, sir. That's all I remember."

Knox nodded and closed the folder. "I hope you know how serious this is, son."

"Yes, sir. I do."

Knox turned to Max Laney. "Mr. Laney, if you wouldn't

mind staying with your grandson, I'm gonna go put in a call to the DA. I wanna make sure we take care of this properly."

He left the room and Laney looked to his grandson. "You just make sure you keep your story straight."

CHAPTER THIRTEEN

We didn't say much on the way back to Hollie's farm. I ran through my options, part of me wanting to stay and avenge Kelly's murder, another part of me wanting to run. The trees rolled by as my thoughts churned. Hollie did the same, never taking his eyes off the road.

As we pulled down the side road leading to the house, I spotted a late model Bronco parked just inside the tree line. I pointed to the trees. "Who lives on that land?"

Hollie glanced that way. "The Baxters. Nice enough. Pretty much stay to themselves."

"Do they own an old Bronco?"

"Not that I remember."

"THANK YOU FOR YOUR TESTIMONY, Mr. Laney. Now, if you'll excuse us, I have to see the judge."

The District Attorney shook Max Laney's hand and nodded to Chief Knox.

Once he'd left, Johnny turned to Knox. "What happens now, Chief?"

"Well, I've gotta wait for the warrant first. Should have that soon. Then we'll see. I appreciate you fessing up, son."

"It's how my granddad raised me. I'm just so sorry." Johnny put his face in his hands, prompting an awkward silence.

Knox rose to go. "Mr. Laney, if y'all wouldn't mind hanging tight, I can have one of the girls run out and get some food."

"That's very nice of you, Darryl, but I think I'll pass. Don't want to overstay my welcome. A coffee would be wonderful though. Black, no sugar."

"Yes, sir. I'll be right back."

The door closed and Laney smiled at his grandson. "Hang in just a bit longer."

———

I TOLD Hollie I wanted to go for a walk to clear my head and come up with a plan. He said he'd do the same while he started on dinner.

It wasn't dark yet, but that didn't matter. I'd been trained to do things in broad daylight without a soul knowing. Leaving from the rear of the house, out of sight of the main road, I jogged a long curving path, finally ending up in the stretch of pine.

Taking a hard left, I moved through the woods, back in my element, thoughts of Camp Lejeune's training grounds in the front of my mind. *Snake Eyes*.

———

I WAS COVERED in sweat by the time the Bronco came into view. I'd snuck in behind the vehicle, senses tingling. Maybe it was nothing, but I wanted to know. A hundred yards away, the driver's side door opened and a man stepped out, walked five feet, unzipped his fly and relieved himself.

There was something familiar about the man, but it wasn't until he turned to step back into the truck that I recognized the sling on his arm. It was one of Johnny's goons.

I weighed my options. Take him down, interrogate him, or let him be. I was torn. This man hadn't done a thing to incur my wrath.

My mind made up, I carefully backed away from the Bronco, retracing my steps back to Hollie's. I'd see how it played out.

––––––

"YOU SURE HE'S THERE?"

"Yeah. Him and Hollie came back. Haven't seen him leave."

"You somewhere that you can't be seen?"

"Just where you told me to be, Johnny, on Baxter's property, across the road."

Johnny looked to his grandfather, who sat listening. "Stay put and make sure the cops don't see you."

"You got it."

Johnny put the phone back in his pocket. "Everything's set."

––––––

HOLLIE GLANCED over his shoulder when I walked in, shirt dark with sweat. "You go for a run?"

"Had to check something out."

"What'd you find?"

"They're watching the place."

Hollie stopped stirring the pot. "Who?"

"The guy with the bad shoulder, from that first morning in the barn."

"Honey?"

"Yeah, I couldn't remember his name. What do you think they're up to?"

Hollie scratched his head. "I don't know, but I don't like it. Come give me a hand with dinner and we'll talk about it."

———

"OKAY, now you all know your jobs. It'll be just like we talked about. I'll go to the door with Al. The rest of you know where to go." Chief Knox waited for questions. There were none. He'd gone over the plan three times. It was not rocket science. "All right then. Let's saddle up."

Twenty men, including two additional officers from the Sheriff's department, stood and walked to their vehicles.

———

WE'D JUST finished dinner when I heard vehicles coming down the gravel drive. It sounded like they were coming fast. "Are you expecting someone?"

Hollie's ears perked up. "Nope. Why don't you go upstairs and I'll see who it is."

———

THE TEN SQUAD cars pulled in front of the house, each passenger out as soon as the driver stopped, moving into their assigned positions. More than one young cop had his finger on a trigger.

———

I CROUCHED next to the window, looking out. They'd sent in the cavalry, but for what? I heard Hollie open the door.

"How can I help you, Chief?" he asked nonchalantly, speaking loudly for my benefit.

"Evening, Mr. Herndon." The chief pulled a wad of paper out of his pocket. "I've got a warrant for the arrest of a suspect in the murder of Kelly Waters."

My stomach clenched.

"Who would that be? Me?" asked Hollie.

"No, sir. We've been told that a man, whose name we do not have, is said to be staying on your farm."

"Well that's news to me son. Wait, you're talking about my friend. He left, hmmm, must have been two days ago."

The chief shuffled nervously, trying to make a decision. "Would you mind if we take a look in your house?"

Hollie laughed. "Actually I would mind. You see," Hollie's voice lowered slightly. "I've got a female guest inside. We were just sitting down to eat when I heard you coming up the drive."

Now the cop looked nervous, glancing at his troops, them looking to him for an order. The shuffling again. "I...uh, can you tell us how we can find your friend?"

"Your guess is as good as mine. He said he was on his way to South Dakota. Wanted to see Mount Rushmore."

"How about his name? Could you tell me his name, Mr. Herndon?"

I strained to hear. Would Hollie lie for me again?

"Of course. I've got nothing to hide. His name is Peter Vallon. Goes by Pete."

The cop pulled a pen out of his shirt pocket, writing the name on the back of the warrant. "Do you have a phone number for Mr. Vallon?"

Hollie chuckled. "Pete's a bit of a hermit. Doesn't do technology. Prefers stopping by to calling. Hell, I didn't even know he was coming until he knocked on the front door."

"May I ask where you met Mr. Vallon?"

"Sure." A pause. "I think it was...hmmm...I'll be damned if I remember. Must be getting old!"

Squinting, the policeman waited for more. "Sorry to bother you, Mr. Herndon. I would recommend calling us if Mr. Vallon contacts you."

"I sure will. Now, if you don't mind, I've got a date to get back to."

Without waiting for permission, Hollie stepped back in the house and shut the door.

After a moment conferring with his troops, more than one of whom looked annoyed, the caravan left the way they'd come. I waited for the police to disappear before coming downstairs.

Hollie was waiting. "Well, at least now we know what Laney's plan is."

I nodded, still wondering why he'd lied for me. He didn't know me. For all he knew, I could have picked up the girl at the bar and killed her. My alibi was tenuous at best. "Who's Peter Vallon?"

Hollie smiled. "An old soldier from Korea. Crazy as a bat on cocaine. Never liked the man. Swear he was stealing from the rest of the platoon. Couldn't prove it. If he's still alive, maybe he'll get a knock on *his* door from the police."

I shook my head, endlessly surprised by the old man's actions. "I guess that settles it. I'll grab my pack and make my way out of town."

"What, and miss the adventure?"

I looked at him like he was out of his mind. "You're kidding, right? Did you see how many cops were out there?"

Hollie waved my comment away. "I'm not worried about them. Darryl Knox is about the biggest idiot I've ever met. He couldn't find his ass with both hands unless he had help."

"What do you think we should do?"

He grinned. "Take the battle to the enemy."

CHAPTER FOURTEEN

Max Laney gritted his teeth, trying to hold his temper. "What do you mean he wasn't there?"

"Mr. Herndon said he left days ago." Knox wiped his blotchy face with the back of his hand.

"And you believed him?"

"I couldn't bust into his house, Mr. Laney."

"You had a warrant!" Laney's temper finally rising.

"It was for the arrest of this Peter Vallon. I can't go searching personal property without the judge signing a new warrant."

Max Laney took deep breaths, counting to ten. As a younger man, he'd freely exhibited his fury, often to terrific effect. After maturing and taking over the family business, he'd worked hard to reform his image. He was a well-respected businessman, and popular figures like Max Laney did not have public temper tantrums.

He knew the man they were trying to frame was still at Hollister Herndon's farm thanks to Honey's surveillance, but he couldn't tell that to Knox.

"You're right. I'm sorry for stepping over the line. You

know what you're doing. If there's anything I can do please call."

Knox relaxed. "Thank you, but totally unnecessary for you to apologize, Mr. Laney. We're all pretty torn up about Kelly."

Max patted the chief on the shoulder. "That we are. Poor girl. Please let her family know that I'd like to pay for all funeral expenses. We'll get her a really nice plot that will do justice to her beauty."

"That's very kind of you. I'll let Mr. Waters know."

————

"WHAT HAPPENED?" Johnny scratched his swollen nose.

Max Laney buckled his seat belt. "It's on us now. How quickly can you get your friends to the house?"

Johnny smiled wickedly. "I'll call them right now."

————

WE SPENT the rest of the daylight hours preparing. If Max Laney and his thugs wanted a fight, we'd be ready. Hollie manned the backhoe as I went about the task of setting out a few surprises for any unwelcome guests.

Hollie parked the backhoe, climbing out gingerly. "I'm headed in. You coming?"

"I've got a couple more. Be in soon."

Hollie turned and headed inside, leaving me to the falling night. My time. I wouldn't be sleeping. Didn't want to. Too many memories. Too much to do.

If the enemy made a move, I wouldn't let Hollie get hurt. I would stand in their way, just as I'd done many times in the past. Silent, alone, waiting.

CHAPTER FIFTEEN

Johnny had rounded up his troops. Most lived in town. Sitting in Max Laney's spacious living room were fifteen guys of varying ages. The majority were Johnny's friends from high school. All had, at one point or another, a run-in or three with the law. It wasn't a stretch to describe them as thugs.

Max Laney mingled with the men who almost bowed to him in deference. To them, Max Laney was a god. Rich, powerful and ruthless. He was the man they wanted to be. He'd promised to compensate them for their time, handsomely.

The plan was to pay a visit to the Herndon farm and take Hollie's houseguest, by force if needed. Max Laney wouldn't take part. He never did, at least not since his twenties.

Johnny walked into the room, a sawed-off shotgun leaning against his shoulder. "We're leaving in five minutes. Grab your shit and get outside." He waited until his men had exited and turned to his grandfather. "I'll take care of the problem."

Laney's eyes steeled. "You better, and remember, we want him alive. He's no good to us dead."

———

THEY CAME JUST BEFORE MIDNIGHT. Typical. If they'd had any tactical training they would've waited until a couple hours before sunrise. It was the best time to assault, even if the enemy was waiting.

I sat in the second story of the barn, night vision scope glued to my eye. "Here they come."

Hollie shifted in the hay next to me. "How many?"

I counted. "Five vehicles."

"Are they spreading out?"

"No. They're coming right down the road."

Hollie grunted.

———

JOHNNY RODE in the fourth vehicle for the simple reason that he'd underestimated the blonde stranger before. For all he knew, the dude could be lying in wait. Johnny Laney wasn't taking any chances. Screw what his granddad had said. If he could get a clear shot, he would take it.

———

THE LEAD VEHICLE cruised over the only rise in the dirt road, it's headlights illuminated the path ahead. The man in the passenger seat squinted, pointing to a patch less than twenty feet ahead. It looked like someone had laid hay on the road.

"What's tha…"

The rest of his words came out in a scream as the front of the truck plunged into the ten foot hole, slamming hard, the second vehicle plowing in right behind.

———

WE'D HOPED to get at least two vehicles out of commission. We got three. The fourth and fifth swerved violently, narrowly missing the trap. I leaned in close to Hollie. "The two others pulled over."

The intent hadn't been to kill anyone. What we wanted was for them to stop and think, and stop and think they did.

———

JOHNNY JUMPED out of the truck, shotgun scanning left and right as if he expected a battalion ambush.

Groans and shouts sounded from the wreckage. Johnny pointed at the mess. "Get those idiots out."

The younger Laney continued to scan the area, wondering what to do next. Too much was riding on the night's impromptu operation. He couldn't fail in his task.

———

I HANDED the scope to Hollie and hopped to my feet. "I'll start phase two."

"You sure you don't want the scope?"

"I'll be fine."

Hollie nodded, looked down at our handiwork, and chuckled.

———

AT LEAST SIX of his men were out of commission with a combination of head and shoulder injuries. Nothing life threatening. "You pussies stay here," growled Johnny. "The rest of you fan out. Same plan as before."

Weapons gripped tightly, the band moved off warily, each man having lost their cockiness.

———

I KNEW they couldn't see me from where they stood, but I sprinted anyway, not wanting to waste a second. It took me just over a minute to set the next part of our production. Smiling, I moved back toward the house, hoping that Hollie would keep his promise and stay out of the way.

———

THE TEN REMAINING toughs moved forward, spread out along fifty yards. Suddenly, up ahead, a spark lit, then caught. *WOOMPH*, went the flames as first one, then two and then three stacks roared to life. Laney's thugs stopped.

———

I COULDN'T SEE the enemy through the flaming hay mounds. Averting my eyes from the glare, I focus on the periphery. My mind wavered, images from the past, screams coming from...

Shaking my head, I settled in, readying my first shot.

———

"KEEP MOVING!" Johnny hissed, more annoyed than scared. He's seen plenty of burning hay bales in his life. If his target wanted to be taken down by the light of their flames, Johnny didn't care.

None of the men walked on the road, and Johnny stayed on the leftmost flank, affording a view of the house. He couldn't wait to put a bullet in someone's head.

———

I LOOKED AT MY WATCH, counting down the seconds to Hollie's cue. Right on time, the booms sounded from the four sticks of dynamite we'd buried in the ground.

———

MOST OF JOHNNY'S men fell to the ground, clods of dirt raining down all around them. Some screamed, one ran back toward the road and more than one pissed their pants. Johnny seethed. *The next motherfucker who pusses out gets a shotgun blast in the face.*

He hissed for the others to get moving. They did so, albeit reluctantly. Johnny strode ahead, marching down the middle of the drive.

———

BREATH IN. Breath out. Slow pull. *BANG.*

———

THE MAN to Johnny's left went down, clutching his stomach. Two more mercenaries turned and ran. Six left standing.

———

BREATH STILL OUT. Shift. Slow pull. *BANG.*

———

NEXT DOWN WAS the guy to Johnny's right. The whole line stopped at the sound of the man's scream.

"This ain't worth it, fellas," said another man. "Let's get the hell out of here."

Three more ran the way they'd come. That left Johnny and the only cousin he'd brought. They looked at each other, and sprinted toward the house.

––––––––

I LOST the shot as the two forms crossed behind a flaming haystack. A form reappeared on the far side, *BANG*.

––––––––

JOHNNY DIDN'T LOOK BACK. He had to find cover and the house was the nearest place. Safety was all he could think of. It never occurred to him that going to the house was what Daniel wanted.

––––––––

I WAVED TO HOLLIE, our signal that it was time for me to head to the house and deal with any stragglers. I'd seen the man's face illuminated. It was Johnny Laney. Just the man I wanted to talk to.

––––––––

JOHNNY'S large frame burst through the screen door, sending him tumbling into the house. He was up in a flash, shotgun searching. It was dark, rays of orange flickering in from the fires outside like some kind of sick horror movie.

"Where are you?!" Johnny screamed, shooting two blasts into the ceiling.

"Right behind you."

––––––––

JOHNNY WHIPPED his weapon around to where I'd been standing a moment before. *BOOM*. I rolled to the side, finding cover behind a couch, the shotgun blasting through the front door.

Pivoting, I grabbed a lamp and heaved it in his general direction, quickly to return in a explosion of glass, my adversary not being a novice with his weapon.

A shadow in the doorway. "Put the gun down, son."

I heard Johnny pivot on the creaky hardwood floor and fire. *BOOM*.

My ears ringing, I poked my head out to where the voice had come from. Hollie lay in the doorway. My world went red, I reverted inward, and attacked.

CHAPTER SIXTEEN

"Like I said, Mr. Laney, we went up there, and all hell rained down. It was like a fucking war zone."

Max Laney stood listening, eyes blazing. "Where is my grandson?"

The scruffy survivor gulped. "He kept going. Lost sight of him after he went into the house."

"And you ran."

"Ye...yes, sir."

Laney turned around. "Get out of my house."

"What about our money?"

"I would have paid if you'd done what you were supposed to do, not run away like a coward."

"But..."

Max Laney whipped around, much faster than his years should've allowed, a pistol aimed at the young man's head. "I said, get out of my house."

CHIEF KNOX RUBBED the sleep from his eyes and grabbed his work phone. "Hello?"

"Sir, it's Simon."

"What the hell time is it?"

"It's just after midnight."

"This better be good."

"We've gotten a couple calls complaining about explosions out by the Herndon farm."

Knox's eyes popped open. "When?"

"A few minutes ago."

"Did you send anyone out there?"

"No, sir. That's why I'm calling you."

"Good. Don't worry about it. Got a call earlier, said the State would be doing some blasting tonight. No big deal. Something about extending utilities, I think."

"In the middle of the night?"

"Like I said, don't worry about it."

The dispatcher hesitated momentarily. "Would you like me to call back the people who called in?"

"That's a good idea, Simon. You might make a decent cop just yet."

"Thank you, sir."

Knox ended the call, setting the phone back on his night stand. He'd gotten a call earlier in the day, but it had been from Max Laney, essentially telling him to turn a blind eye. Darryl Knox did what he was told. He owed Max Laney too much.

Without another thought on the topic, he rolled over and was asleep in less than a minute.

———

HANDS COVERED IN BLOOD, I ran over to Hollie. "Hollie, Hollie, are you okay?"

He groaned, moving his right arm. "I think he just winged me. Shitty shot just like his granddaddy."

I breathed a sigh of relief, having feared the worst. After turning on the lights, I inspected Hollie's arm. "I think you're right. Your left arm's bleeding pretty badly." Looking around, I grabbed a clean shirt from the stack of laundry I'd folded earlier in the day.

"Damn that hurts." Hollie watched as I did my best to stem the blood flow. "You do this before?"

I nodded.

"Afghanistan?"

Another nod. "That should do it until we can get you to the hospital."

With more strength than I expected, the old man sat up. "First things first. What are you gonna do with him?"

I looked at the bloody form across the room. Johnny Laney lay in a puddle of his own blood. I winced at the sight, recognizing the carnage left by the skills I'd acquired in my past life. The assault remained a blur. I'd acted on instinct. Luckily, unlike before, this time I'd stopped short of killing the man.

"Help me up. We've got work to do."

Standing up, I reached down and helped Hollie. Cleanup time.

CHAPTER SEVENTEEN

Max Laney paced, a crystal tumbler in hand, his third. There hadn't been a word from his grandson. The rest of the cowards had apparently scattered leaving him without a way of knowing what happened.

A series of honks sounded from the front yard. Laney walked to the entryway, one hand still gripping his pistol. Some vehicle moved slowly up the drive. Squinting, he realized it was Johnny's truck. "Finally."

Laney opened the front door and stepped outside, waiting. The truck kept coming, then ran over a part of the perfectly manicured shrubbery, still rolling forward. He couldn't see through the high beams, attempting to shield his eyes with a hand.

The truck missed part of curb cruising right through the dew covered grass. It wasn't stopping. Frantically, Max Laney moved aside as Johnny's truck made a bee line for the front door, finally ramming into the structure, crumbling brick and dry wall as it went. The pickup stopped, engine still revving.

Cautiously, weapon extended, Max Laney approached the

vehicle. There was a burlap sheet bound over the truck bed. He ignored it and moved to the cab seeing the back of someone's head in the driver's seat.

"Put your hands up!" yelled Laney.

No response.

"I said, put your hands up!"

Nothing.

Moving in an exaggerated crouch, Laney closed the remaining distance, flinging the driver's side door open. He looked down his gun sight to see Johnny, face badly beaten, his entire front covered in blood, duct taped to the steering wheel, foot stuck to the accelerator.

Laney's eyes went wide, one hand shooting up to check for a pulse. Alive.

Next, his composure regained, he moved back to the truck bed. Someone had secured the burlap with what looked like parachord. Laney quickly untied one end and flung the sheet back. Piled inside like firewood were three of Johnny's crew, duct taped like mummies and just starting to regain consciousness.

————

"WHAT DO you think he'll do?"

Hollie shrugged, causing him to wince. "I guess we'll see."

We'd just left Max Laney his package and were headed to a 24-hour clinic a town away. The official story would be that I'd accidentally shot him. It sounded ridiculous to both of us, but like Hollie said, "People will believe most anything you tell them as long as you say it with a straight face."

He was right. No one batted an eye when Hollie checked himself in at the emergency clinic. All procedure. It made me wonder how many firearm accidents they handled annually.

The only downside was that they asked for Hollie's next of kin, of which he had none, and I volunteered to give my name. They checked it against my worn military ID card, and not another word was said.

CHAPTER EIGHTEEN

They called a physician who was part of Laney's extended family. He wasn't happy about the late night visit, but he couldn't say no. Max Laney was the one who'd co-signed for his medical school loan. It wasn't the first time the favor had been called.

"I think Johnny got the worst of it. Lacerations to the face and he may have a broken cheekbone. How did you say this happened?"

Max Laney frowned. "I didn't. Can you take care of him here?"

"I'd highly recommend he at least get an x-ray..."

"I said, can you take care of him here?"

The doctor nodded slowly, ready to say anything to get away from the lunatic. "I'll have to put in a few stitches, and I can write up a prescription for some pain meds."

"Fine. How about the others?" Laney pointed at the three men sitting nervously around the kitchen table.

"Looks like it was some kind of tranquilizer dart. I would've been worried if they hadn't woken up, but since they're up, the full effects should wear off by sunrise."

Laney nodded and the three men breathed a sigh of relief. Each one had thought they'd died taking a bullet in the raid.

"Can we go now, Mr. Laney?" one of the three dared to ask.

He got a curt nod in response. They didn't waste a second in leaving.

———

I DROVE the truck slowly up the drive, taking in the wreckage in the pit we'd dug hours before. "That was a great idea."

"We did a lot of that in Korea. Stupid Communists would roll right down the road, not taking a second look and bam, the first vehicle dropped the column stopping with them. You were the one that got us out with the hay bale idea and your shooting."

I chuckled. "It didn't hurt that you just happened to have a tranquilizer gun lying around along with a few sticks of dynamite."

"What can I say? I was a boy scout growing up. Be prepared, right?"

"Right."

Hollie yawned. "When it gets light out we can pull those trucks out and fill the hole in."

"You don't think Laney will try it again?"

"Max Laney is a mean son-of-a-bitch, but he's not stupid. I'll bet my life that he'll try something else. We just have to be ready."

At that moment, I had no idea how we were going to get ourselves out of the mess.

———

THIRTY THREE STITCHES LATER, the doctor departed. No

thanks was given as he walked out the kitchen door, the front door still an impassable mess.

Laney stood over his grandson, arms crossed. "Tell me everything, from the beginning."

"Come on, granddad. Can't I go to bed?"

"You'll sit there and tell me what happened or I'll smack you around myself. Now, tell me."

Johnny huffed and retold the story.

"YOU SURE YOU SHOT HOLLIE?" asked Laney, after listening to each detail intently. He had to give it to the two, they'd caught him by surprise. That didn't happen, ever.

"Yeah. Came in the front door and I shot him."

"Do you think you killed him?"

"I don't know. After I saw him fall, the other guy... He was like an animal. I couldn't stop him."

Laney seethed. "You had a shotgun and you couldn't take down an unarmed man?"

"I...I can't explain it. It was something in his eyes. I could see that he was going to kill me."

"But he didn't."

Johnny didn't have a response. Truthfully, he was scared. He'd expected a simple in and out. Instead, he had encountered a demon. The implications rushed through his mind as he tried to shake the feeling of unease. Laney saw the look on his grandson's face. "Snap out of it! He's just a man! Do you know how many men I've killed?!"

Johnny nodded, looking away.

Laney grabbed him by the chin, blood squeezing out of the gauze bandage. "He's dead, you hear me? One way or another, he's dead."

———

I HELPED HOLLIE INTO BED. He didn't complain once. Tough old soldier. "Good night."

"Good night, Daniel. Good work tonight."

"I'm not so sure about that."

Hollie's eyes opened, appraising me. "You did the right thing, son. Nobody got killed and you didn't hurt anyone that didn't deserve it."

"Maybe we should've called the police."

"Maybe, but that's water under the bridge. We're men. We made our beds and now we have to lay in them. I'll tell you this, I don't regret a single thing."

I pointed to his bandaged arm. "You sure?"

"I had a lot of worse in the Army. Now stop beating yourself up about this. You're a good man. I believe in you. Besides, it felt good being in an ambush again. Reminded me of my time in the Army."

Forcing a smile, I patted him on his good hand. "Get some sleep. I'll keep a lookout."

Hollie suddenly seemed much older as he closed his eyes, fading to sleep instantly.

I watched his breathing, standing sentinel still. Finally, I clicked off the overhead light and left the room, floor creaks following me outside.

The smell of burnt hay still hung in the air, rekindling old memories, thoughts I didn't want to have. I grabbed Hollie's Garand from the front porch, checked the chamber and settled in one of the adirondack chairs. It would be another sleepless night. Snake Eyes took up his post, waiting, ready for the enemy. Even awake, sitting in the dark, the nightmares came, like moths to a flame.

CHAPTER NINETEEN

The sun had barely cracked the horizon, and a construction crew was already hard at work repairing the Laney complex. Max Laney watched the work, sipping an espresso, planning his day. He'd made two appointments, the first of which he would soon be leaving for.

The phone buzzed in his linen pant pocket.

"Laney."

"Mr. Laney, it's Darryl Knox."

"What is it, chief? I'm a little busy."

"Yes, sir. Well, I just got some news that I thought you might like to hear."

"Yes?"

"Got a call this morning from a colleague in Santa Rosa Beach. You see, we get reports of gunshot wounds from clinics and hospitals."

"Can you please get to the point?"

"Yes, sir. My friend called to give me a heads-up that Mr. Herndon got checked out early this morning at a twenty-four hour clinic in Santa Rosa."

"And?"

"He listed his next-of-kin as a Daniel Briggs."

Laney smiled. "Good work, Darryl. I assume you're looking into this Mr. Briggs?"

"We are."

"Good. You let me know what you find out. Come up with anything good and I'll throw in an all expenses paid vacation for you."

Laney ended the call before Knox could trip over himself.

"Daniel Briggs."

———

I WAS DRAGGING by the time I heard Hollie moving around inside. There hadn't been a lot of sleep in the preceding days. I knew I was reaching my limit. I'd have to sleep sometime, but I dreaded it.

Hollie opened what was left of the front door. "You hungry?"

"I'll make breakfast. You take a seat out here."

"Won't complain about that."

I could see he was in pain. I'd never been shot, but I knew plenty of people who had. They always said I was indestructible because I always seemed to walk away without a scratch. If they could only see my soul. I felt more like a bad luck charm.

"Eggs and toast okay?"

Hollie nodded, grimacing as he eased into the porch chair.

I BROUGHT breakfast out for Hollie and we sat eating quietly, enjoying the uncharacteristically cool morning.

Hollie sniffed the air. "Storm's coming."

Looking up at the sky, I couldn't disagree. You could feel the drop in barometric pressure.

He put his plate on the ground. "I was thinking about how they found Kelly in Rosemary Beach. How do you think she got there?"

"Probably drifted."

"I don't know if it'll help, but I've got a boat docked in Panama City Beach. Wonder if it might be good idea to take a gander."

"What do you think we'd find?"

"Not sure, but I know the Laneys have a couple boats down there too. Might be good to take a look around."

"I don't know if you should be taking that chance."

"What, and let you have all the fun? I'm old, not dead, Marine."

It was hard to argue with the man. Old or not, he was still a warrior.

———

MAX LANEY LOOKED over his silver sunglasses. "You got all that?"

"Yes, sir."

"Do you foresee any problems?"

"I've never failed, Mr. Laney. I don't plan on it now."

Laney handed the slight man with bushy eyebrows a padded manila envelope. "Here's the first half. You get the rest when you're done."

———

IT TOOK the better part of an hour to get to the boat dock, beach tourists starting to clog the roadways. "Is it always like this?"

Hollie stared out the window. "During spring break and summer. I try to avoid it when I can."

"What do you have a boat for?"

"Fishing mostly. Sometimes it's nice to take a ride. My wife loved to cruise along the coast. I can still see her smiling like a child. She loved it."

He hadn't said much about his wife. There were still mementos of her touch in his house, mostly pictures and furniture, stuff a man wouldn't buy. "If I can ask, what happened to her?"

His gaze never left the ocean. "Cancer. Five years ago. We found out pretty late. She lived two months after the doctor diagnosed her."

"I'm sorry."

Hollie turned and looked at me. "So am I. There isn't a day that goes by that I don't miss her. She made me whole. I almost died when she left."

"I can't imagine."

He cocked his head. "I think you can."

"What do you mean?"

"I can see you, Daniel Briggs. You're a tough Marine, probably a sniper or force recon. But you're human. I see your pain. It's okay if you don't want to talk to me about it, but there will come a day, hopefully not long from now, when you will have to tell someone, deal with the demons."

I didn't want to hear it. My temper flared. "What do you know about it?"

Hollie chuckled. "Son, there are things that I've seen that I never told a soul. Tore me apart inside for a long time. Did I tell you that I lost half my platoon in Korea?"

My hands gripped the steering wheel hard, the memories bubbling to the surface. I couldn't speak for fear of letting my emotions run.

"I blamed myself for a long time," he continued. "Wasn't a soul I could talk to. I thought no one would understand. Hurt a lot of people because of my anger. Fell hard, privately, of course. Everyone else saw a hero coming home after saving the world from the North Koreans. I felt like screaming at them. Drank a lot in those days. Tried to forget. Hurt my friends. Hurt my family."

I tried to steady my breath, focused on the road.

———

IT HADN'T BEEN HARD for Renley Watts to find the old man's place. He'd almost missed them. From years of practice, he hung back, his borrowed 2002 Honda Accord blending well once they hit town. Tracking was simply a matter of pulling up next to the pickup, arm dangling out the driver's side window, and tossing a magnetic tracking device against the old man's truck.

The hard work done, Watts sped off to find a secluded spot to park and begin monitoring his quarry.

CHAPTER TWENTY

We pulled into the Bay Point Marina after driving past the community golf course.

"Nice place," I admired, taking in the variety of boats sitting in their wells.

"I'm over on the left."

———

"THEY JUST PULLED into the Bay Point Marina."

Max Laney scowled. "What are they doing?"

"I'm not there yet."

"Well hurry and get there."

"I will."

———

THE FIRST STOP was Hollie's boat, a twenty two foot center console fishing rig named *Bite Me*. I pointed to the name. Hollie laughed. "A little joke between me and my wife. She hated sharks and I always used to kid her about them. The name was my lame attempt of humor."

We climbed aboard, Hollie inspecting as he went.

"Know anything about boats?" he asked, using a towel to wipe the bugs off the console.

"Got my coxswain's license in North Carolina, but that was a while ago. Probably couldn't tie a knot if you asked me."

"But you know how to drive?"

"I do."

"Good. Come over here and give me a hand."

———

RENLEY WATTS PULLED into the Marina casually, taking his time. It took him a minute to find the truck. Seconds later, he spotted Daniel's head peeking out of the white fishing boat.

Parking a ways off, but still with a view of the two men, Watts settled in and watched.

———

HOLLIE HAD JUST FINISHED his obligatory maintenance checks. "What do you say we take her out for a spin?"

"I was thinking about going over to the shop and asking around. Maybe someone saw Johnny the night Kelly was killed."

"Good idea. I'll come with you."

THE GIRL behind the counter was completely unhelpful. Her eyes were glued to the old television in the corner.

"Are you sure there wasn't anyone here that night?" I asked, starting to lose my patience.

"Yes, sir. Like I said, owners can access their boats

twenty-four hours a day. Gas and electric are self-service. We don't staff this place all night."

"What about security cameras?"

She finally looked up at me. "Are you a cop or something?"

Hollie nudged me. "No, ma'am. We're just looking for a friend who was supposed to meet us."

There was a pause as she pondered clamming up. "What's his name?"

"Johnny Laney."

Another pause, and then she rolled her chair over to the computer. "You tell anybody I did this and I'll swear you threatened me."

"Don't worry, this stays between the three of us." Hollie threw me a wink.

A few keystrokes later she looked up. "Says he got some gas at two in the morning, the night you were looking for. Does that help?"

"It does. Would you mind telling us which well he was in? I can't remember the name of the boat."

She huffed and swiveled back to the computer. A few keystrokes later she said, "The Midas Touch. Well 341."

———

"THEY JUST WENT into the tackle shop and now they're headed to...they're going back to the old man's boat."

"Get out and see," order Laney.

"I can't. There's no one around. If I go, it'll be too obvious."

"Just do it!"

———

WE FOUND THE BOAT, and with Hollie playing lookout, I

climbed aboard. The thing must have been at least sixty feet in length. It was the nicest vessel I'd ever been on.

It didn't take me long to find what I was looking for.

———

"YEAH, they're on a boat called The Midas Touch."

"What did you say?"

"I said, the kid just climbed onto a boat called The Midas Touch, blue trim, chrome portals."

Laney mind swirled. That was his boat, but it wasn't in the right place. He had docked it a week earlier in a friend's slip across the bay. Occasionally he used the Bay Point Marina, but only when he wanted to shack up with a part-time girlfriend he kept who owned a condo across the street.

"Keep an eye on them."

Max Laney clenched his hands as he walked down the hallway to where Johnny lay recuperating.

———

I HOPPED DOWN, landing nimbly on the concrete dock. "Let's go."

"What'd you find?"

"I'll tell you in the truck."

Hollie followed as I led the way, mind frothing. Familiar contingencies running through my head. Once again operational.

"What did you see?" Hollie asked, after we'd pulled out of the parking spot.

I told him.

———

MAX LANEY SLAMMED Johnny's bedroom door open. The prostrate form didn't move. Anger boiling over, he marched to the bed, looking down at his pathetic excuse for a grandson. Grabbing a Playboy magazine lying on the ground, Laney rolled it up tightly and swung, connecting over and over again against Johnny's stitched and bandaged face.

His grandson was soon yelling, curled in a ball, trying to protect his face.

"You lying sack of shit! Fucking worthless...son-of-a..." The beating continued, this time against the back of the head.

"What the hell?!"

Out of breath, Max Laney threw the magazine against the far wall. "Last chance...you tell me...how did you do it?"

Johnny, hands still protecting his face, rolled over slowly. "What are you talking about?"

"That girl...how did you kill her...how did...?"

"Are you okay, granddad?"

Laney leaned against the wall. "I'm fine. Just out of breath. Now tell me."

"I already did."

"You said you strangled her and drove to Grayton Beach Park and dropped her in the water."

"That's what..."

"Don't lie to me!"

"I...I don't remember. I woke up at the Park and drove home."

"I'll tell you what happened! You took *my* boat, drove into the Gulf, obviously not far enough, didn't weigh her down, and then docked the fucking boat at Bay Point Marina!"

Johnny sat up, confusion setting in. He couldn't remember. "What do you want me to do?"

Max Laney's eyes bulged. "The first thing you're going to do is get down to that marina and clean up your mess!"

A LOOK of horror on Hollie's face. "My God. I knew he was messed up as a kid, what with his dad dying and his mom overdosing, but this is...poor Kelly. The news didn't say anything about..."

"Why would they? You don't advertise that stuff." The scene in the cabin replayed in my head, on repeat. Blood, so much blood. "This changes everything."

"What do you mean?"

"Our plan was to get Johnny to confess or find enough evidence to bring to the police."

"And?"

"He doesn't deserve it."

Hollies face darkened. "Where are you going with this, Daniel?"

My vision cleared. Mind working with body. A finely crafted instrument. "All the way."

CHAPTER TWENTY-ONE

"You sure you don't want me to follow them?" Watts was already in his car, idling.

"Stay there. My grandson will be at the boat soon. I need you to babysit him."

"I don't know, Mr. Laney. That's not really..."

"Do it, keep your mouth shut, and I'll double your fee."

Watts's mouth snapped closed. A double fee meant he could postpone the three shitty jobs he had waiting. "Done."

JOHNNY LOOKED like Frankenstein after facial reconstruction surgery when he stepped out of his truck, trying to find his grandfather's boat.

Watts whistled quietly. *Now there's a piece of work.* He'd never met Johnny, had only heard about him from Max and the rumors through the grapevine. It was Renley Watts's business to know about his clients. He knew about the assault charges, drug arrests and DUIs. All dismissed thanks to the Laney tie to the police department. Watts wondered how much his employer paid the police chief. He made a mental note to do a little snooping, maybe he could use it as leverage to increase his future payments.

Watts caught up to Johnny just as he was climbing aboard. "Mr. Laney?"

Johnny's head whipped around. "Who the fuck are you?"

"Your grandfather sent me, said he'd given you a call."

He had. Rather than reply, Johnny grunted and climbed the rest of the way onto the boat, Watts followed.

"Oh, shit," came the groan from the main cabin. Watts went that way, stepping lightly down the stairs, hand on his hip holster. His eyes went wide coming into the spacious main room. Disgust turned to glee as Watts made up his mind that Max Laney would have to pay him ten times his normal fee to keep quiet.

―――――

LANEY WAS ONLY HALF LISTENING to the general contractor, his mind still replaying the phone conversation with Renley Watts. Deep inside he wasn't surprised. Johnny had always been disturbed. He'd once caught then seven-year-old Johnny strangling the family dog, a lovable Bichon, just for the fun of it. When asked why he'd done it Johnny had replied, "Because I could."

The years hadn't improved his grandson's attitude, although he'd gotten better at hiding his indiscretions. He'd had to pay countless thousands to pay-off the local police, buy new cars and have enforcers keep witnesses, who wouldn't take payment, quiet.

"I'm sorry, Tom. Can we do this later? I've got a lot on my plate today."

"No problem, Mr. Laney."

Laney went back into the kitchen, rooting through drawers looking for his trusty headache powder.

"Mr. Laney?" It was the contractor again.

Laney bit his tongue, not wanting to snap at the man. "What is it?"

"There are two gentlemen at the front door who said they'd like to speak to you."

Laney ignored the headache. "Did they say who they were?"

"No, sir. There's an old guy with a bandage on his arm, and a young guy with blonde hair."

Laney panicked for moment, then calmed. If they'd wanted to hurt him, they wouldn't have walked in the front door and announced themselves.

"Please tell them I'll be right out."

He felt stupid for not keeping security at the house, but Max Laney was no coward. He'd stared death in the face numerous times and come out alive. He could take care of himself.

———

MAX LANEY STROLLED out like a king. I could tell he had a gun in his pocket. "Hollie, Mr. Briggs, how can I help you today?"

The sound of my name coming out of his mouth made me cringe. He knew who I was.

I looked around at the workers busy rebuilding the mess we'd made the night before. "Let's talk out back."

Laney nodded and led the way, nonchalantly turning his back to my piercing eyes.

Walking out onto the stone-paved back patio, Laney took a seat. "Can I offer you anything?"

"You can tell me where Johnny is."

"Why should I do that, Mr. Briggs?"

I matched his stare, imagining cramming by boot up his stuck-up ass. "So I can kill him."

Laney shook his head. "So barbaric. Why would you want to kill my grandson?"

"You know why."

"I'm not sure I do."

Hollie stepped in. "Cut the crap, Max. You know he killed the Waters girl. Hell, you even tried to frame Daniel for the crime."

Laney's facial expression never changed. "I really hate to disappoint you both, but I have no intention of handing over my grandson, but...if you would consider payment in exchange..."

I took a quick step closer. "I don't want your fucking money, asshole. Keep playing your little games and maybe I'll take care of you too."

"Tsk, tsk, tsk. I don't think that would be very smart, Mr. Briggs." He pointed toward the front yard. "Lots of witnesses saw you come in here. I'm a public figure. I disappear and people will start asking questions. No, I think what's going to happen is that you are going to get off my property before I call the police, and give them every bit of evidence that will tie you to the murder scene."

I smiled "Not *every* piece of evidence."

I'll give him credit, he didn't flinch. "What do you think you have?"

"I don't *think* I have anything. I know that there's a video, in my possession, that shows your sick grandson raping, maiming and then murdering Kelly Waters."

"You're bluffing."

"Try me."

Silence.

"What do you want?"

"I told you, I want Johnny."

"I already..."

"I know, I know. Family first. Let me put it this way, wouldn't it be better to give up your twisted excuse for a grandson, saving yourself years of cleaning up his mess, and keeping your empire intact? If that video surfaces your pals will disappear. Everything you've built will be torn down."

I could see his scheming mind weighing his options. He wasn't stupid. Max Laney lived a very comfortable life. "Very well. What do you want me to do?"

CHAPTER TWENTY-TWO

Johnny went straight to his room to shower. He was tired. A beer and a nap was what he needed.

"Thought you could avoid me?" came Max Laney's voice from behind.

Johnny turned around, wearily. "No, sir."

"Did you clean up the mess?"

"Yes, sir."

"Where's Watts?"

"He'll be here soon. Said he had to stop for gas."

It took every ounce of self control in Laney's body to not lash out at his pathetic offspring. "Do you know anything about a video?"

Johnny's face went blank. "What video?"

Idiot. "Nevermind. Take a shower and get some sleep. We have a meeting tonight."

"With who?"

"Someone who can make all this go away."

Johnny brightened at the revelation. "Great. What time do we leave?"

———

"ABSOLUTELY NOT. I'm going with you."

"Hollie, I can't risk it. Trust me, I know what I'm doing."

Hollie shook his head emphatically. "You know how many times I've heard someone say that before doing something stupid?"

I couldn't help but laugh. "Yeah, me too. Listen, if this thing goes south, I want you safe. Besides, you'll need to turn that video in if I don't make it back."

Hollie glanced at the video camera I'd taken from Laney's boat and shivered. "Okay, but you're going prepared."

"I always do."

———

MAX LANEY WASN'T HAPPY, but had finally met Watts halfway on his fee. It now sat in the passenger seat, neatly stacked in a brown paper grocery bag. Even better, Laney had another request, one that Renley Watts was only too happy to deliver.

Watts flicked on his windshield wipers, looking up at the darkened sky. The storm would be overhead soon. Watts made a mental note to stop and buy a rain coat. The night would be wet.

———

IT'S YOUR FAULT! It's your fault! I bolted upright, the ghostly image still wavering before me.

"You okay?"

I looked over at Hollie. We'd decided to take quick naps. Any sleep was better than no sleep. "Yeah." I rubbed my fingers on my eyes. The rain was really coming down, thunder in the distance. Good and bad for what I was planning.

"You sure you want to do this tonight? That's storm's gonna make it tough."

I shrugged. "Nothing I haven't done before."

THIRTY MINUTES, two cups of coffee, and a bologna sandwich later, I grabbed my pack and headed to the door.

Hollie followed. "Got everything you need?"

"I do."

"How will I know if everything goes off right?"

"I'll see you in the morning."

Hollie frowned, but stuck out his good hand. "Good luck, Marine."

———

"LET'S get on the road. I don't want to be late."

Johnny nodded and opened the door for his grandfather, who was dressed casually in jeans and work boots. He'd told Johnny to wear something comfortable, and to grab a rain coat.

They drove slowly down the drive, water already rushing across cutting lines in their path. "Where to, granddad?"

"Take a right. We're going back to the boat."

Johnny did as he was told, anxious to be done with the ordeal, the most embarrassing of his life. He'd already promised himself that he'd clean up his act and become the man his grandfather needed. "Yes, sir." Johnny turned onto the paved road, rain pounding into the windshield.

———

EVERYTHING LOOKED GOOD. I double and triple checked the gear. I was soaked, but the summer heat still lingered, perfect weather.

Navigation lights on, engine purring, I backed Hollie's boat out of the well. A flash of lightening struck a mile away illuminating the way momentarily. Now pointed into the bay, I slowly increased speed, relishing the thrumming rain.

CHAPTER TWENTY-THREE

The roiling waves slammed repeatedly into the boat's hull, punctuating the storm's anger. "You sure you know where we're going, granddad?"

Max Laney looked down at his GPS, a marker showing the rendezvous point in green. "We'll be there soon."

Johnny tried to see out, only catching a glimpse of the Gulf when lightening flashed. "Seems like a crazy place to meet up."

Laney ignored him, focused on the way ahead.

———

I SAT BOBBING FOR AN HOUR, waiting. Finally, a set of navigation lights came into view. Flashlight in hand, I blinked in the boat's direction three times. A pause, then the flashes were echoed. On cue, every light on Laney's boat came on.

Two figures stood in the illuminated wheelhouse.

———

Max Laney pointed to the controls. "Wait here. Keep us steady."

"But, who's..."

"I said, stay here. I'll be right back."

Laney, already wearing his all-weather coat, climbed out onto the deck.

———

I could barely see Laney's face, still trying to keep Hollie's boat from coming too close to the other.

"What now, Briggs?"

"I'll throw you a rope. Have Johnny tie it around himself. He'll have to jump in the water."

Laney nodded, bracing himself on the railing as another wave rocked him back. "I'll get him."

So far so good.

———

"Strip down."

Johnny looked up in confusion. "What?"

"Strip down to your skivvies. You're going for a swim."

"You're kidding. I can't go out in *that*."

Laney sighed. "Johnny, this is the only way. The man on that boat is the only one that can get you out of this mess. Now, would you rather go for a swim or go to jail?"

Johnny didn't know what to say. He'd expected a quiet dinner. Instead, his grandfather had brought him out into the middle of the Gulf, storm raging, then asked him to swim out to a stranger's boat. "But..."

"You don't have a choice. It's this or you're cut off."

Johnny stared at his grandfather, waiting for the punchline. None came. Reluctantly, he began stripping off his clothes until he stood in only his boxer briefs.

Max Laney turned to go. "Come on."

Johnny, wide-eyed, somehow managed to put one foot in front of the other.

LANEY STEPPED out onto the deck again, Johnny following behind, his pale body shivering in the rain. It wasn't cold, but he looked scared. I wondered what his grandfather had told him. He didn't seem to recognize me from the distance.

Carefully maneuvering into position, I grabbed the rope that sat coiled on the console, one end already secured to a cleat. The waves threatened to smash the two vessels together, so rather than risk a collision, I sat back at a distance I figured I could throw the rope. Worst case, Johnny would have to swim a little bit to snag it.

"Jump in!" I called over the storm.

Johnny looked to his grandfather, who motioned to the angry ocean. The nearly naked man shuffled to edge, muscles clenched.

"I said, jump!"

I stood ready to throw, not wanting to have to make another pass. Johnny ducked between the railing, feet on the edge of the rocking boat. He was trying to time the swells, not wanting to get swept under the boat.

Another bolt of lightning struck, thunder simultaneously booming. A shadow in the corner of my eye. I turned, squinting. Suddenly, a spotlight blinded me, then another. Two more boats had snuck up in the night. I cursed under my breath.

As I went to gun my throttle, gunfire erupted from the

two newcomers, multiple flashes, followed by the pings as they hit my boat. I ducked for cover, the familiar feel of rounds overhead.

One round, then two hit the outboard motor, I felt the power slacken and the boats came closer, never letting up with their firing. I counted at least six shooters, maybe seven.

More hits, the glass above my head shattered. I ignored it, still focused forward. Motor sputtering, waves pounding. Another lightning strike up ahead. I could smell the gas despite the hard rain blanketing my movement and the sea water lapping over the side.

Power fading, and with the three boats close behind, I turned the wheel so that the boat was no longer headed into the waves but running parallel. A huge wave crashed over the side almost sending me into the sea. I gripped the wheel with all my strength, rounds still hitting all around. The boat rolled over the opposite side of the wave, literally gliding into the mouth of the next. Just as I looked up at the cresting behemoth, an explosion blew me through what was left of the windshield, and sent me sprawling into the bow of the boat. As I turned to regain my footing, the wave crashed down.

———

MAX LANEY ORDERED THE MEN, led by Renley Watts, to keep firing. There wasn't much left of the craft, the burning engines already having been swallowed by the sea.

They stayed for another thirty minutes, passing to and fro, spotlights searching the water. Nothing. No sign of the boat or of Briggs.

Laney was satisfied. Maybe Briggs had survived the explosion, and maybe he hadn't been drowned by the capsizing boat, but no one would survive near hurricane conditions two miles out to sea.

Max Laney signaled for the others to head in. Their work was done.

CHAPTER TWENTY-FOUR

Hollie sat waiting, rifle sitting in his lap, pointing toward the door. He hadn't heard from Daniel yet and was worried. It had been hours since the Marine had left. Hollie said a prayer, asking for his friend's safe return.

A light in the distance made Hollie lean closer to the window. There was a vehicle coming up the drive. The old Army Ranger controlled his heart rate with deep breaths, watching the headlights. He'd learned to distinguish most cars and trucks by their lights, and these looked familiar.

Hollie squinted. It was his truck, bumping up the gravel road. Hollie breathed a sigh of relief. "Thank you, Lord."

Rising to meet his friend, Hollie flipped on the front porch light. He stepped outside and waved. His pickup pulled into its parking spot and the driver got out, waving back to Hollie. Then three men stood up in the bed of the truck, weapons pointed in his direction. The driver who'd now thrown back the hood of his rain coat, also had a gun pointed at Hollie. "Put the rifle down!"

For the first time in his life, Hollister Herndon relinquished his weapon, and surrendered, his heart broken for the loss of another comrade.

———

"WHY DIDN'T you tell me what your plan was?"

Johnny had whined the whole way home, making Max Laney think that maybe he should have given his grandson to Briggs.

"I told you, I didn't want to give it away. You wouldn't have been that scared just by acting. I had to throw Briggs off. Now quit crying. You're fine."

Johnny mumbled something under his breath, wringing his hands in the towel he'd taken from the boat. "So is it over?"

Laney grinned. "Watts says he's got Hollie and the video camera at the house. We'll be finished tonight."

The younger Laney breathed a sigh of relief. It had been a long couple of days. He looked forward to things getting back to normal, having a cold beer, getting laid. "What are you gonna do with Hollie?"

"I'm not sure yet, but I might let you have him when I'm finished."

Johnny grinned wickedly, relishing the thought.

———

HOLLIE DIDN'T SAY a word as he was led into the Laney complex. He knew what was coming, but wasn't scared. He'd lived a good life, married his high school sweetheart, had a son, worked hard. Everybody's time came at some point. His only regret was Daniel. He thought that maybe if he'd pushed the young man to leave, or taken the evidence to the police, that Daniel would now be on his way to another town.

But that wasn't the case. Renley Watts had already told him about Daniel. Like so many he'd known before, Hollie mourned silently for his dead friend. Another Marine dead before his time. A kid with so much left to give.

Hollie was shaken from his thoughts at the sound of pounding footsteps coming down the hall.

"Where is he?"

"In the living room."

Max Laney stormed into the room, drenched, but smiling from ear to ear. "Well look who it is. Our old friend, Hollister Herndon."

Johnny walked in right behind, looking grotesque with wounds still raw and bandages peeling. "Let me have a little fun, granddad."

"Not yet. I need to have a word with Mr. Herndon first." Laney turned to Watts, who stood watching. "Your money's in a bag in the front closet. Johnny will show you out."

Watts followed Johnny to the front door as Max Laney took a seat in front of Hollie. "Now, let's get down to business."

"I think I'm done talking. Kill me and get it over with."

Laney laughed. "I'm not going to kill you...yet. We've got business to discuss."

"What kind of business?"

"You're one of the last holdouts in town. I control most of the land around here except yours. You've had a good run, but I think it's time for you to retire from farming. If you play nice, and deed the property over to me, I might be able to overlook our recent...disagreements."

Hollie glared. "Over my dead body."

"Let's not go there, old friend."

Johnny walked back into the room. "Can I have him now?"

Laney's eyes narrowed with annoyance. "Can't you see I'm talking?"

Johnny closed his mouth, crossed his arms, and waited.

Brushing a piece of lint off the side table, Laney continued. "My attorney will be here in the morning. Hopefully by then you'll have changed your mind. If you're pleasant I might even give you a decent price."

"Go to hell."

"In time, I'm sure. Johnny, why don't you take him to the basement and loosen him up a bit." Johnny grinned. "But don't make it too obvious. I want him to be able to talk and sign his name."

"Yes, sir." Johnny walked over to Hollie, placed his left hand on the old man's shoulder, and without warning, slammed his right fist into Hollie's gut, doubling him over. "That's just the start, old man."

CHAPTER TWENTY-FIVE

The storm still raged when morning came. Flash flood warnings were in effect for the entire Florida Panhandle area, and not set to expire for more than a day.

Chief Darryl Knox drove carefully through town, avoiding the raging torrents that had engulfed large chunks of pavement. His staff had already been to the scenes of nine traffic accidents, one involving a bus full of churchgoers. No one had been hurt, but the wreck had clogged traffic for miles.

Despite all that was happening, Knox had an errand to run. He'd called Max Laney as early as he'd dared, not wanting to incur his benefactor's wrath again.

Pulling into the roundabout in front of the Laney home, Knox's eyes took in the restoration that was underway, the workers away probably because of the rain.

Knox managed to get to the front stoop without his umbrella turning inside out. He knocked. A moment later, Max Laney answer the door, still wearing stylish pajamas.

"Good morning, Chief."

"Morning, Mr. Laney. Thank you for having me."

Laney ushered him into the house, where Knox respect-fully removed his shoes and left them by the front door.

"What is so important that you had to drive out here in the storm?"

Knox opened his oversized coat and pulled out a file he had tucked under his arm. "I got some more information on Daniel Briggs and thought you might like to see it."

Laney's eyebrow rose. He almost told Knox that he shouldn't have bothered, but was curious. "Why don't we go in the kitchen. Can I get you a cup of coffee?"

"Yes, please. Cream and extra sugar."

While Laney got the chief's coffee, Knox sat down at the kitchen table and opened the folder.

"What did you find?"

"I think you were right, Mr. Laney. Mr. Briggs is a very dangerous man."

Laney set the coffee down in front of Knox. "What do you mean?"

"Well, I did some calling around, had to pull some strings with an old buddy of mine in St. Louis, but I finally got the guy's military records."

"Military?"

"Yes, sir. He's a former Marine, actually he was a sniper."

"So he was...I mean *is* dangerous."

Knox nodded. "He left the Marine Corps a couple months ago. Spent a lot of time overseas. Some of his stuff was censored and not even my buddy could recover it, but the information he did give me describes a very interesting char-acter, someone who knows how to kill."

Laney slid the file over, scanning the documents. *Honor graduate from Parris Island. Scout sniper. Meritorious promotion to Lance Corporal. Meritorious promotion to Corporal. One tour in Afghanistan. Five confirmed kills. One tour in Iraq. Twelve confirmed kills. One tour in Afghanistan. Recommended for...*

Laney looked up. "He was recommended for the Congressional Medal of Honor?"

"That's what it looks like, but if you read further, you'll see that he also suffers from post traumatic stress disorder after his last tour in Afghanistan. I think that held up the confirmation proceedings."

Marine sniper. Medal of Honor. The words rattled around in Laney's head, breeding doubt, not for what he'd done, and not for killing a hero, but...

"Based on this information I think we should alert the Marine Corps and the FBI, as a courtesy."

"Let's see how this plays out first, chief. No need to scare the whole town. I suggest you conduct a thorough investigation, keep it quiet, then reap the rewards once he's in custody. You'll be a hero."

Knox nodded, thoughts floating on clouds of glory. "That sounds like a good plan, Mr. Laney. I sure do appreciate you letting me run this by you."

"Any time, chief."

———

HOLLIE SPIT out another gob of blood, a trickle running down his chin. Johnny had worked him over well, careful to inflict the damage on the old man's torso, avoiding his face. Hollie was pretty sure he had at least two broken ribs. The stabbing pain came with every breath.

He was alone in the basement. They hadn't bothered gagging him, knowing that the reinforced structure kept all sound in the bunker-like complex. Bound to a steel chair, Hollie, rendered useless, could only hope the end would come soon.

CHAPTER TWENTY-SIX

The attorney, Henry Ellison, arrived just before lunch time, driving up in a modest Cadillac De Ville. Renley Watts, back on duty at the Laney compound, met the lawyer at the front door and led him in to see his boss.

Max Laney rose from the table. "Henry, so good of you to come." The two men embraced.

"You know I'm around whenever you need me, Max."

Laney clapped his old friend on the back fondly. "When do I get to take your money on the golf course?"

Henry Ellison chuckled. "I'm getting too old for golf. My back's not what it used to be. Besides, you've got me too busy working. Speaking of which, did you really convince Hollie to sell?"

"I did. We came to an arrangement. Did you bring all the paperwork? I want this to be quick and easy. Hollie isn't feeling well."

"I didn't know that."

"Mr. Watts, can you fetch Mr. Herndon for us?"

"Yes, sir."

Watts left to get the prisoner, who'd already been given

new clothes and a swift clean-up. Watts couldn't wait to see what happened next. His respect and admiration for the Max Laney's cunning had only increased over the preceding days. Watts hoped it would be the beginning of mutually beneficial relationship.

———

THEY'D WARNED him not to make a scene. It took every ounce of control for Hollie to hold his tongue when shaking Henry Ellison's hand. He knew the attorney to be an honest and hard-working man, who'd been duped into believing Laney's lies for the last thirty years.

"I heard you've been a little under the weather, Hollie. Everything okay?" There was genuine concern in the attorney's tone.

"Just getting' old. I'll be fine."

"We'll keep this quick. Mr. Laney's already signed everything. I'll give you a summary. Feel free to ask any questions you might have."

Hollie nodded and took a seat, feeling Laney's stare burning into him.

Ellison proceeded to explain the quit-claim deed, and how the transaction would transpire. Hollie wanted to vomit. His whole life's work, the sweat and toil of generations of Herndons, gone with the swipe of a pen.

TRUE TO HIS WORD, the paperwork took less than ten minutes. Smiling from ear to ear, the attorney shook everyone's hands, gathered the legal documents and headed back out into the storm.

Max Laney patted Hollie on the back. "See, that wasn't so hard."

Now that the lawyer was gone, Hollie's head hung, tears falling into his hands. "Are we done here?"

"We are."

———

RENLEY WATTS RETURNED from securing Hollie in the basement. "What now, Mr. Laney?"

Laney puffed a well-deserved cigar, ignoring his latest health kick, enjoying the pungent taste on his tongue. It had been a productive day. The fee he'd have to pay Watts was a small price to pay to gain control of the Herndon estate. "Take care of Mr. Herndon."

"Yes, sir. You want me to do it now?"

"Wait until the storm dies down, then have Johnny take you out in the boat."

Watts was being paid twice his annual income to do Laney's dirty work, and he loved it. He hadn't had as much fun in years.

CHAPTER TWENTY-SEVEN

The storm hadn't subsided by the time dusk came. Watts was anxious to get paid. "I don't mind going now, Mr. Laney."

"I'm still waiting on Mr. Ellison to call and confirm the transaction was recorded with the state. Last thing I want is for some government employee to need one more signature and Hollie's at the bottom of the ocean."

"So...Mr. Ellison doesn't know anything about your... extracurricular activities?"

Laney stared daggers at the hired gun. He was beginning to have second thoughts on hiring the man again. Watts had his uses, but something about him made Laney uneasy. It was prudent to keep such men at arm's length. Watts already knew too much. "Henry Ellison and I go back to our toddler days. He is a fine and upstanding lawyer, as honest as the day is long. My father once told me that there are only two things a businessman needs, God and a damned good lawyer."

Watts smiled. Hearing his employer talk of God made him want to laugh. He and Laney were cut of the same cloth.

Do what you need to do to get the job done. "You just tell me when."

————

AN HOUR LATER, Max Laney had finally lost patience and placed a call to his attorney's office. The secretary answered, "Ellison and Garvey."

"Max Laney for Mr. Ellison please."

"I'm sorry, Mr. Laney, but Mr. Ellison isn't back yet. We thought that maybe he was still with you."

"Um, no. He left hours ago. Maybe he had other appointments?"

"No, sir. Mr. Ellison had us cancel the rest of his appointments when he scheduled yours."

Laney stared at the wall. "Well, when he gets in will you please have him give me a call?"

"Yes, sir."

Henry Ellison missing. Maybe it was the storm.

Laney dialed another number.

"Defuniak Springs Police," answered the dispatcher.

"Max Laney for Chief Knox, please."

————

DARRYL KNOX WAS JUST SITTING down for dinner when his phone rang. He groaned when he saw it was dispatch. It had been a long day dealing with the havoc caused by the storm. "I thought I told you I was busy for the next two hours."

"Yes, sir, but I've got Mr. Laney on the line. He says it's an emergency."

Knox put his glass down and got up from the table, motioning for his date to continue eating. Once in the lobby, Knox asked for Laney to be patched through.

"Chief Knox."

"Chief, I'm sorry to bother you."

"Not a problem, Mr. Laney. How can I help?"

"Do you now Henry Ellison?"

"The attorney?"

"Yes. Mr. Ellison was here earlier in the day, and I've been waiting for his call. I just talked to his office and they say he never returned. I wonder if maybe he ran off the road somewhere."

"It's been happening all day. I can't remember the last time we had to call Eddy's Towing so many times."

"Would it be possible for you to send out a couple units to look for him? He's a very old friend. I would hate it if anything happened to him."

Knox closed his eyes, taking a deep breath, wishing he could get back to dinner. "I'll get right on it, Mr. Laney."

———

PATROL CARS SCOURED the routes to and from the Laney residence, spotlights shining off the roadways. They found Henry Ellison's car an hour after beginning their search. Chief Knox called Max Laney from the scene.

"We found Mr. Ellison's car."

"Is he okay?"

"He's not in the car, Mr. Laney. The first officer on the scene found the car off the road, crashed into a tree. The driver's side door was open, but no sign of Mr. Ellison."

Laney's face paled. Of course he was concerned for his friend, but he was more concerned with the purchase contract. He'd already transferred funds into a pair of Hollie's accounts to make the deal seem legit, despite the low price. "Was there...anything in the car? Any sign of him?"

"We searched it inside and out. Nothing. Couldn't even find a footprint what with the rain and all. I'm about to have the boys start looking in the woods. Maybe he wandered off and got lost."

"Please hurry. I'm scared to think of what might happen to him."

"We'll do everything possible. I'll let you know as soon as I can."

Laney stood in silence, save the pounding rain. Where was Henry Ellison?

———

LIGHTS FLASHED in the dreary night, trying vainly to cut through the darkness and sheets of rain. They called out as they walked, methodically sweeping the area.

"I've got something!" came the shout.

Darryl Knox sloshed his way toward the voice, the others continuing the search. "What have you got?"

The officer pointed with his flashlight. "Looks like a white suit coat."

It was pointless trying to take pictures in the rain. Besides, it wasn't a murder investigation. Knox bent down to search the coat. On the inside pocket, clearly stitched was *Henry Ellison, Jr.*

"Dammit."

"Is it his, chief?"

"It is. Now keep looking."

The cop moved off to continue the sweep. Knox peered into the soup, hoping they'd find the old lawyer soon.

———

HOLLIE'S HEAD lolled to the side at the sound of the basement door opening. Max Laney walked in a moment later, a look of disgust plastered on his face.

"Looks like this is your lucky day, Hollie."

A look of confusion. Hollie had expected his executioner. "What are you talking about?"

"Well, there's been a little...delay in getting the paperwork processed. That means that you'll live to see another day. I thought I'd bring you the good news."

"Why should I care?"

Laney shrugged. "Thought a Godly man like yourself might like to enjoy his last hours on earth. It's a gift."

Hollie laughed out loud. "You fucking hypocrite. Get out my sight. You mention God again and I might puke on your pretty little shoes."

Pulling a chair over, Laney took a seat across from his captive. "Very well. I'm bored. How about we chat a bit?"

"I don't want to talk to you."

"Not even about Mr. Briggs, the Marine sniper?"

Hollie's glared. "Don't you dare."

"What? Can't we honor his memory? Such a hero and all? Seems only fitting..."

"You don't deserve to talk about that boy. He was a good kid and you had him killed."

Laney nodded thoughtfully, almost sadly. "That's true. He might have been a mighty foe. I'm sure you were proud of his being nominated for the Medal of Honor?"

The look of confusion on Hollie's face said it all.

"You didn't know?" Laney's devilish smile spreading. Hollie shook his head, the tears coming again. "That's too bad. I wonder why he didn't tell you. Why do you think that is?" Not a word from Hollie. "Maybe you weren't as close as you let on. Did you know about his PTSD?"

The sobs started. Hollie coughed up more blood, moaning like a man who'd just lost his wife.

Laney went to put a comforting hand on the man's shoulder, but thought better of it. He stood up. "Well, at least that should give you something to think about. Max Laney not only took your land, but killed your hero friend. How fitting."

He turned and headed to the stairs, leaving Hollie to his searing grief.

CHAPTER TWENTY-EIGHT

After three hours of traipsing through soppy fields and obsidian woods, Chief Knox called the search off. They'd try again in the morning, possibly calling in the search dogs from the sheriff's office.

Knox sat in his car, eyes closed, heat blasting, trying to warm his shivering body. Despite being summer, the hours of trudging in the rain had taken a toll on everyone, the out of shape Knox more than the rest. A knock on the window.

It was one of his officers. Knox reluctantly rolled down the window three inches. "What is it?"

"You want us back at the office?"

What Knox wanted was a hot meal and a shower. "Tell everyone to go home, get some shut eye, and meet up just after sunrise."

"You got it, chief."

Knox rolled the window up, once again relishing the hot air coming out of the vents. He waited for the rest of the cruisers to leave and placed a call to Max Laney, his fifth of the night.

"Did you find him?"

Knox exhaled, exhausted. "We didn't. I'm sending the boys home and we'll head back out in the daylight." He waited for a reply, wondering what Laney was thinking.

"Thank you for trying. Please let me know if there is anything I can do."

"I will, Mr. Laney. Have a good night."

Knox threw the phone on the passenger seat and shifted the car into drive. A very hot shower was calling.

———

MAX LANEY WAS as close to panicking as he'd been in years, maybe decades. His plans had flown with the disappearance of Henry Ellison.

Renley Watts watched the old man pace, wondering what his next move would be. He was ready to serve as needed, for a price. Why not make a rich deal even more lucrative? "How can I help, Mr. Laney?"

His employer looked up in surprise, having forgotten Watts standing in the corner. "I'm not sure there's much we can do tonight. I've left a message with Ellison's firm, they'll get new paperwork out here in the morning with or without Henry."

"So you need Herndon to stick around?"

"Of course, you idiot. We'll have to re-sign everything. I can't do that without him." Laney slammed his palm on the granite countertop. "Dammit."

———

HOLLIE WALLOWED IN MISERY, second-guessing his actions. *I should have let him leave.* The guilt weighed heavily on his sore shoulders. He wanted to die.

Forgive me, Lord.

CHAPTER TWENTY-NINE

Max Laney rose before sunrise. He'd become accustomed to functioning on little sleep, mostly with the help of repeated bladder calls during the night. What he would have paid for the body he'd once had.

Sipping an espresso, he looked up when Johnny walked in, hours before his normal wakeup.

"Morning, granddad."

"You're up early."

Johnny grabbed a coffee mug. "Thought you might need some help. What can I do?"

Laney hadn't expected Johnny's sudden turn. The previous night Johnny had kept his mouth shut, doing his best to be useful. "Why don't you get Hollie something to eat and drink. I don't want him to pass out when the lawyer gets here."

Johnny sipped his coffee. "Did they find Mr. Ellison?"

"No. Knox said they're going back out this morning. I was thinking about heading out there later."

"Want me to come with you? I can drive."

Laney motioned his grandson closer, lowering his voice. "I want you to stay here and keep an eye on Watts."

Johnny's eyebrows rose. "Why?"

Laney shook his head. "He's getting a little full of himself. Asking a lot of questions. I don't trust him. He knows too much. Your only job is to watch him and make sure he's not getting in the way."

"Yes, sir."

Maybe he could have Johnny kill the man. It wouldn't hurt to get the ludicrous amount of cash back that he'd paid the mercenary. Max Laney smiled, the pieces coming together in his head.

———

POLICE OFFICERS TRICKLED into the office, all tired from the previous night's search. They drank coffee and devoured donuts waiting for Chief Knox to arrive. He was usually a couple minutes late, but thirty minutes was pushing it. More than one person wondered aloud whether the chief was still asleep.

———

MAX LANEY PULLED his SUV off the road, looking down to where Henry Ellison's Cadillac still sat, surrounded by yellow police tape. Knox and his men weren't there yet. Laney waited, counting down the minutes, listening to the rain beating down.

———

"YOU THINK I SHOULD CALL HIM?" asked one of the Defuniak Springs cops.

"I already did. No answer."

"That's not like the chief. I'm gonna drive over to his

place. Maybe he forgot to charge his phone again."

The others laughed. Chief Knox was not known for his tech savvy. He often asked his deputies to type a text for him in reply to a message from his on-again off-again girlfriends.

"Take your time. I'm in no rush to walk around in that rain again."

More laughing as they continued to wait.

———

HE'D SAT for close to an hour before calling Knox. The lawyer would be at the house in thirty minutes. Laney's patience was paper thin as he listened to the ringing on the other end, Chief Knox's voicemail message finally played. Ending the call, Laney dialed the police station.

"Defuniak Springs police."

"This is Max Laney for Chief Knox."

"I'm sorry, Mr. Laney. The chief isn't in yet."

"He told me last night that there would be a search party out in the morning to look for Henry Ellison."

"Yes, sir. We've been waiting for him. Just sent an officer to his house. I think he slept through his alarm."

Laney counted to ten, breathing slowly, trying to stay calm. "Will you please have the chief call me when he gets in?"

"Yes, sir."

Henry Ellison and now Darryl Knox. Both missing.

He dialed Watts.

"Watts here."

"I need you to meet me...now."

———

JOHNNY LOOKED IN THE MIRROR, moving his head from side

to side. His wounds would heal. It was his pride that had taken a beating.

His grandfather had tried to groom him to take over the family business for years, but he'd always taken it for granted. After his father's death, he'd moved into the position to inherit the family fortune.

The past week had shown Johnny that his future as head of the family was in jeopardy. He liked his life and didn't want it to change. Things would be even better when he took over.

A knock on the bathroom door.

"I'm in here."

"Hey, it's Renley. Your granddad just called, I'm heading out to meet him."

"Hold on."

Johnny wiped a dribble of blood from his chin with a wad of toilet paper, chucking it into the trash when he was done. He opened the door.

"Where is he?"

"He's where they found the lawyer's car."

"What does that have to do with me?"

Renley rolled his eyes. Max Laney he could deal with. Johnny not so much. "Just keep an eye on Herndon, okay?"

"I'm not an idiot."

"I didn't say that, I...never mind."

Johnny watched the man go. Maybe his grandfather would let him tear the pig apart soon. He had to get his pent up aggression out somehow.

———

WATTS PULLED up next to Laney's SUV fifteen minutes later. He hurried through the downpour and hopped in the passenger side door. "Where are the cops?"

"Looking for the chief."

"What happened?"

Laney told him what he knew.

"You think they're telling the truth?" asked Watts.

"Of course. What I can't figure out is what happened to Knox."

"Could he be shacked up with a girlfriend? I've heard he's got a couple."

"It's possible. I want you to find him."

"What about Herndon?"

"Johnny can take care of him until you get back."

Watts wanted to protest, hoping to stay close to the action and the likelihood of making more money. He held his tongue. "Any ideas on where I should start?"

Laney frowned. "Isn't that *your* job?"

Watts sighed with a nod. "I'll get right on it."

"And be quick about it! Something's not right here."

Watts couldn't disagree.

CHAPTER THIRTY

The police found Chief Knox's squad car in a ditch now overflowing with water. Knox wasn't in the car and there weren't any signs of where he'd gone.

Just as they'd done the night before for Henry Ellison, the officers donned their rain gear and went searching for their boss.

———

"IN A DITCH?" Max Laney stared out the window incredulously. What else could the storm throw at him?

"Yes, sir. They're looking for him now. I just thought you'd like to know," said the dispatcher.

"Okay. Thank you."

Laney was late for his meeting. Johnny called to say the new attorney was waiting. He'd instructed his grandson to make sure Hollie looked presentable and not to lay a hand on him.

"I'll take care of it, granddad."

At least Johnny was one less thing he had to worry about.

Maybe he would get his shit together. He hadn't told Johnny, but he'd recently taken steps to have the entire family business pass on to a cousin in Ft. Walton Beach, a man ten-years Laney's junior, but a savvy financial advisor. Only time would tell whether Johnny could regain his full favor.

Just as he went to pickup his phone, a shadow passed across his peripheral vision. Laney's head snapped left. Nothing, but then again, he could barely see a thing through the driving rain. He slid his revolver out of his pocket, just in case. *Probably a bird.*

Wary, Laney shifted the SUV into reverse, making sure his four wheel drive was still engaged. As the vehicle rolled back, a clod of mud hit the windshield, making Laney jump. He pressed the brake, engaging the wipers, trying to see out, holding the revolver tight.

It was impossible to see more than a ten feet into the murk. *What the...* Another pile of mud hit the back window. Laney didn't wait. Trusting the off road capabilities of the SUV, he stomped on the gas. Tires spun, trying to get a hold in the slick ground. *BOOM! BOOM!* Laney felt the front of the cross-over drop, followed by the low tire pressure warning lights pinging on.

He didn't dare get out of the vehicle despite his growing concern. Whoever was out there was either trying to get him to come out or...

A figure, dark, more hulking than human, moved closer, patiently. Laney pointed his weapon shakily at the shadow gauging the distance. Suddenly, the figure dropped out of sight.

Frantic, Laney tried to get a better view, pressing the gas pedal, the SUV refusing to move.

BOOM! BOOM! The back end dropped again preceding the flicker of warning light from the tire at the rear of the vehicle.

Laney cursed, dialing 911 as he scanned through the rain blasted windows.

BOOM! BOOM! Laney ducked. "Who are you?!" he screamed.

Nothing but the sound of the storm answered. Another dinging and a red flashing lights on the dash. Whoever had taken the shots hit the engine, causing a drop in multiple fluid pressures.

"Hello?" It was the voice of the 911 operator.

"Uh...yes, this is Max..."

BOOM! BOOM! Cowering, Laney whispered into the phone. "Someone just shot out all my tires and my engine. I'm stuck and there's a maniac..."

"Where are you, sir?"

Laney told her.

"I've dispatched the local police, sir. Are you safely inside your vehicle?"

"I'm in my vehicle, but I'm not fucking safe!"

"Can you describe the person outside the vehicle?"

"No godammit! It looks like a swamp monster!"

Laney couldn't stop his hands from trembling. He couldn't remember ever feeling so helpless. His bladder threatened to expel its contents.

"Sir, the police are two minutes away. I suggest you stay in the vehicle until they arrive."

Max Laney almost laughed. There wasn't a way in hell he was going to get out.

———

"HE SAYS he saw the swamp thing?" the police officer asked the 911 operator.

"Something like that."

"First the chief disappears and now the swamp thing is on the loose."

"Tell me about it. I've had more phone calls today than I've had in six months. Let me tell Mr. Laney you're almost there."

———

"Sir, can you see the police cruiser?"

"Yes, I can see their lights now."

"I'll stay on the line until they make contact with you."

The flashing lights approached causing Laney to breathe a small sigh of relief. He observed two officers getting out of their vehicle, one with a pistol, the other with a shotgun extended. They moved cautiously, creeping closer.

Finally, after what seemed like an eternity, one of the officers tapped the driver's side window. Laney rolled it down.

"Are you okay, sir?"

"There's a lunatic out there. Be careful."

"We're checking it out now, sir. If you would, please stay in the vehicle until we clear the area."

Laney nodded and closed the window, watching as the two men looked all around, even under the SUV. Head shakes.

Minutes later, their inspection complete, the same officer tapped on the window. "Did you see which way your attacker went, sir?"

"No. I saw him for a second..."

"So it was a man?"

"I...I'm not sure. Like I told the lady on the phone, it looked like some kind of swamp beast. It was too far for me to get a good look, then it started shooting."

The officer looked at him like he was drunk. "And you're sure it was gunfire you heard?"

Laney almost lost his cool, turning crimson. "Yes. I know what gunshots sound like."

Again the unsure look from the cop. "Okay, but we haven't seen any visible damage other than your flat tires."

"And how do you think they got that way, and for that matter, how did my engine die?"

The policeman shrugged, spilling rainwater into the window and landing on Max Laney's lap. "If you'd like, you can move over to the cruiser."

"No, thank you. I'll stay here until you've cleared the area."

"Suit yourself. We've got another squad car coming with a tow truck. We'll have you out of here thirty minutes tops." The officer turned to join his partner, but glanced back. "Is there anyone you could think of who would want to do this to you, Mr. Laney?"

There was a laundry list of enemies from the past. It was hard to choose one. "Not that I can think of."

As the officer left to write his report, Laney sat thinking, and shaking.

CHAPTER THIRTY-ONE

Max Laney slammed the front door shut and stomped into his house. Between searching the area and taking his statement, it had taken over two hours for the police to get him home. There had been no sign of his attacker, though they had found two bullet holes under the engine compartment when the towing company finally got the SUV on the lift.

"Granddad?" Johnny came around the corner, his eyes going wide at his grandfather's appearance. In stark contrast to his usual slick put-togetherness, Max Laney looked like he'd been dragged through the mud, literally.

"Is the lawyer still here?"

"He said he had another appointment and that he'd be back this afternoon if it worked for you."

Laney glowered at his grandson. "I told you to keep him here."

"He was here for almost three hours. When I couldn't get you on your phone I figured this afternoon might work better."

Rather than continue the conversation, Laney kicked off

his loafers and walked into the kitchen. He needed a stiff drink badly.

———

RENLEY WATTS HAD SPENT the morning calling on anyone who might've known where Chief Knox was, using the same story in each case. He'd avoided the chief's home, assuming correctly that the police had already been there.

There hadn't been another call from Laney, and he didn't want to phone his employer unless he knew more. Hopefully that would be soon. Watts was getting tired of knocking on doors like a beat cop.

"Thank you, ma'am. Would you please call if you hear from Chief Knox?" Watts handed the woman his card.

The slightly overweight redhead, who Watts judged to be in her late forties, batted her disproportioned eyes. "I sure will."

Watts forced a smile and went to leave.

"Hey, you didn't say what you wanted to talk to Darryl for."

Watts turned back, flashing a grin. "Oh nothing serious, and don't say anything, but it seems that a distant cousin won some money in the lottery and he wants to gift a portion of it to Mr. Knox."

Girlfriend #3 licked her lips. "Mmm. Don't worry, I won't tell a soul."

Watts doubted it, but didn't say so. He'd come across all sorts over the years. It didn't take him long to figure people out. This one was most definitely a divorcee, money hungry, and begging for sex. Knox's other girlfriends had been the same. Watts figured it was the only way a moron like Knox could get laid. Flash a badge and some cash.

He thanked the woman again and left the apartment

complex. Max Laney would be pissed if he didn't call, but Watts was over caring. He had his money and would take his time. Maybe another raise was due.

MAX LANEY EXAMINED the paperwork the attorney had left. He couldn't sign it until the man returned, and served as a witness, but Laney was nothing if not a thorough man. The morning's excursion had shaken his resolve. He needed to focus on business to clear his mind of the uncomfortable fear that had ruffled his nerves earlier.

Johnny walked into the kitchen wearing a collared shirt with khaki pants that were a little too tight. At least he was trying. "Have you heard from Watts?"

"Not yet."

"What about the cops? Have they found anything?"

Laney slammed his fist on the table. "Can't you see I'm busy?!"

Johnny frowned, and he put his head down like a wounded puppy. "Sorry. Just trying to help."

Laney exhaled. "It's okay. I appreciate you trying. It's just that...well, this isn't quite how I planned things."

"I know. I haven't helped things either. I swear, I promise to be better. I know I've said that before, but this time it's for real. You can count on me, granddad."

Laney looked up at his grandson and nodded. "Okay. If you want to help, sit down and I'll explain what I'm reading. You'll be in charge soon."

The comment brightened Johnny's mood. He took a seat and listened to the ins and outs of the real estate transaction.

HOLLIE HAD LOST all track of time. The grief was his only companion, teasing him, pointing a finger. He was sore all over. The pain was the only thing that kept him conscious. Part of him just wanted to pass out, or die. But Hollister Herndon was made of tougher stuff than most men. He'd survived a war. He'd survived the loss of his only son. He's survived the death of his wife.

Suddenly, for some inexplicable reason, he raised his head. A warmth he couldn't understand spread from his head down his body, tingling. His mind cleared. He had survived. He wouldn't go quietly.

Saying a prayer of thanks, Hollie refocused his thoughts. Somehow he would make Max Laney's life miserable, even if it killed him in the process. Hollie smiled.

CHAPTER THIRTY-TWO

The power had gone out twice as Laney quizzed his grandson, the storm showing no sign of slowing. Trees swayed ominously, some bending like a bowed fishing pole, threatening to snap.

Laney's phone rang. It was Watts. "Laney."

"Mr. Laney, it's Renley Watts. I've pretty much exhausted everything I could think of. There's still no sign of Chief Knox. Have you heard anything from the police?"

"No. They've called every hour with an update. The storm is making it impossible to bring in more help. The governor's already declared a state of emergency for the entire panhandle."

"Yeah, I just heard about that. The roads are pretty bad. Not many people out."

Unable to think of an alternative, Laney said, "Come back to my place. I'll need you here when the lawyer arrives."

"Yes, sir. I'll head that way now."

Laney put the phone down. "Now, where were we?"

Watts pulled a U-turn, crossing over the deserted intersection, sending rushing water in waves. He'd purchased a police scanner at a local pawn shop after visiting Knox's last girlfriend. He listened to the chatter intently, hoping to glean something, anything, that could help.

Instead of progress in the search for their chief or Henry Ellison, the cops reported accident after accident. Cars in ditches. Trucks sliding into creeks that were now rivers. Too many idiots were still trying to drive in the crappy weather.

Watts laughed, glad that he'd left the police force years ago. He'd never liked being a peon. Going private had been exciting, if not challenging. There had been good and bad years. Watts wasn't a businessman, but he was good at what he did, namely finding and using information for gain.

He schemed as he drove, calculating how far he could go with the scoop he had on the Laneys. Watts wanted to latch himself to a steady train, giving him more income stability . Max Laney could be the answer.

As Watts daydreamed, he kept his eyes on the road, maintaining a safe driving speed as he turned onto one of the country roads leading to Laney's house. The last thing he needed was to run off the road like Knox and Ellison. Just as he had the thought, he spotted a fallen tree laying across the road, not fifteen feet in front of him. Watts pressed the brakes, skidding to a halt.

"Shit."

There wasn't a way around. Watts huffed, putting his car in park. After a moment to think, he got out of the car, instantly drenched by the deluge. The tree was too big to move. Someone would have to take a chainsaw to the twelve-inch thick trunk.

Watts turned to get back in the car, cursing his luck. Just as he opened the door, he felt a presence behind him, a shadow out of the corner of his eyes. Before he could pivot around, a blinding pain spiked the back of his head, followed by darkness.

———

JOHNNY BALANCED a plate in one hand as he closed the basement door. He'd been surprised at Hollie's attitude. The crying had finally stopped, and for some reason he looked...hopeful.

The doorbell rang as Johnny made it to the top of the stairs. "I'll get it."

Not taking any chances, he pulled out the pistol from his waistband and peeked through the window by the front door. He couldn't see anything for a moment, then he noticed Watts's car parked next to his truck.

Johnny looked through the peephole of the new reinforced door. There wasn't anyone there. His face crinkled in confusion. *Where is Watts?* He opened the door, his opposite hand still gripping the pistol, and looked out. His eyes fell to the ground. He took a hesitant step back, inhaling sharply, shutting the door. "Granddad!"

———

"DO you want me to call the police?" asked Johnny.

Laney stared down at Renley Watts's body, his dead eye's bulging, the jagged tree branch the size of a man's wrist buried deep in the man's throat. It hadn't been a pleasant death. Laney wondered if Watts died from asphyxiation or internal bleeding first.

Whoever had dropped the body on the front porch hadn't stuck around to say hello. The warning bells in Laney's head raged.

"Don't call the police. They might think we did it. Get on

your phone and get as many of your friends here as you can. We'll need the help."

Johnny kept looking out of windows already having gone around the house to make sure no one had busted in. No breach so far. "What about the body? We can't just leave it here."

"Don't you think I know that? Call your friends. Tell them to come armed."

As Johnny went to make his phone calls, Laney scoured his mind for a solution. He had to find out who was toying with him. His thoughts drifted back to the night in the Gulf when he'd concluded his business with Daniel Briggs. *Could it be?* Laney shook the ridiculous feeling away. Even if the Marine had somehow survived the capsizing boat, there was no way he could've made the swim to shore, over two miles, and then found his way back to Defuniak Springs. Surely it wasn't possible. Still, the feeling nagged at Laney.

———

A DARK FORM moved along the tree line, more beast than human. Its movements were fluid like a panther stalking prey. It slithered around the perimeter of the Laney compound stopping here and there. The only thing visible in the tangle of grime and debris covering the figure's form were two eyes, almost snake-like.

CHAPTER THIRTY-THREE

Lightning crashed into the woods less than a mile away, thunder following a moment later. The sound shook the house. Without warning the power went out.

Laney looked up, waiting for the power to return. It didn't.

Johnny had managed to contact some of his buddies, nineteen of whom agreed to make their way over. The rest had either never replied to his text or come up with some excuse. Laney made a mental note to recruit more help for the future.

"Call the power company and see if they can get a crew out here," he ordered Johnny.

He listened to the conversation already knowing the outcome. They were too busy. There had been a thought in the past of installing a gas generator, but he'd put it off. What he wouldn't give for it now.

Another thunder clap rattled the windows making both Laneys flinch.

"That was close," Johnny said, on hold with the power company.

A crash somewhere upstairs. It sounded like maybe one of the huge trees near the house had finally fallen.

"Go see what that was."

Johnny nodded nervously, handing his phone to his grandfather, his other hand palming a pistol. "I'll be right back."

Laney ended the call with the power company, knowing they were on their own until the storm settled down. He sat with his back to the wall, a Mossberg tactical shotgun pointing forward, half expecting the strange shadow from earlier to come creeping around the corner.

Two minutes passed, then five. No Johnny. "Johnny! Everything okay?"

No response. Laney stood, weapon at the ready. The first thing he noticed was the smell, swampy, almost like mildew. Peeking around the corner he had to squint in the dark to see mud spots leading from the stairs. He couldn't tell where they started, but he could see where they led; toward the basement door.

Trying to steady his breathing, Laney crept along the wall, moving slowly, scanning. Despite straining his hearing to detect the intruder, the storm drowned out everything.

"Johnny!" he called again. Still no answer, only the repeated crash of thunder.

Still shuffling, Laney reached the door leading downstairs, weapon pointed at the open portal. He went for the light switch before remembering that the power was still out. Pulling out his phone, he turned on the flashlight app and held it against the shotgun so both the light and the barrel were pointing down the stairs.

He followed the tracks further, no marks on the wall, but it looked like something had been dragged. The door at the bottom of the stairs was open. The light from his phone tried in vain to cut into the darkness below.

Counting to three, Laney burst into the room, swiveling

all around, trying to find a target in the pitch black. Nothing except Hollie's figure in the chair.

Still scanning left and right, he approached where Hollie had been for almost a full day. "Hollie," he whispered.

No response.

He could see that the man wasn't moving. Maybe he'd passed out by the looks of how he was leaning back. The beam from his phone leading the way, Laney tried to focus on Hollie. Something wasn't right. It...

Bathed in blueish light sat his grandson, obviously dead, a jagged tree branch sprouting from his eye socket.

CHAPTER THIRTY-FOUR

I was no longer human. Growling and grunting instead of speaking. All feeling had left my body. I thought and moved on instinct, a cunning mind no longer my own. Like a mighty beast, my focus narrow, body in perfect harmony. I gave in.

The small part of my humanity had been pushed to the farthest reaches of my consciousness. Morality no longer mattered.

No words left my lips. No emotion registered in my eyes.

Hollie followed wordlessly, sensing my change. He'd tried to engage me in conversation when I stepped into the basement. I couldn't. Instead, I'd dragged Johnny's lifeless body, untied Hollie from his bonds and replaced him with with the man I'd just murdered. Hollie watched in silence.

Whatever part of me that still existed told me to get Hollie to safety. I listened to the tiny voice much like a dog might listen to its master. Obey without a thought. Move when you're told. Now.

After slipping out the first story window like a cat, I helped Hollie ease down to the ground. Still without speaking, I handed him the keys to the car in the drive, the one owned by the man who I'd killed on the road. Somehow I'd known him to be connected to my enemy. How does a guard dog know who to attack or who to care for? It just does. It smells evil. It senses the enemy.

It was like having a finger on the pulse of the universe. I knew without looking where my enemy was. He was within reach, and yet, I did not attack, sensing that it was not yet the time.

I kept my eye on the house as Hollie drove away, me standing in the rain. A face appeared in a first story window. He saw me. I stared. He screamed. I stood.

Bored with the exchange, I turned and melted into the storm.

———

MAX LANEY SCREAMED over and over at the figure in the distance, finally understanding what had come to pass and who had done it. His legacy lay dead in the basement. Utter despair...then a switch clicked. Even if was the last thing he did on earth, he would kill Daniel Briggs.

CHAPTER THIRTY-FIVE

Max Laney left his grandson's body where it was, not wanting to scare the reinforcements. They came in waves. Half had been on the ill-fated excursion to Hollie's farm nights before. The other half were more curious, and hungry for money. He'd promised them each a small fortune.

"Now that we've got everyone here, let me tell you what we're gonna do."

———

JAW SET, eyes on the road, Hollister Herndon's mind churned. In the past hour his world had turned upside down. Daniel was alive. Johnny was dead. While the image of the mud and tangle camouflaged Marine surprised him for a moment, it was what Daniel had become that was most disturbing.

He'd seen it before. Men pushed to the brink, whose lives no longer mattered. These men were often seen as heroes, but Hollie knew better. Yes, what they did could be heroic, but the detachment turned them into something else, something primal. Hollie knew that's what Daniel was.

But it didn't bother him. He knew the young man's heart. In the short time they'd known each other the Marine had shown Hollie a true warrior. Against all odds, Daniel returned from the dead seeking vengeance. Hollie would help him now, and God willing, after.

———

THE BAYING of hounds preceded the first group to leave Laney's estate. He'd called in a favor to have a local dog trainer, who supplied to law enforcement across the country, to bring his full contingent. Max Laney had agreed to not only pay the man's hefty fee, but to also compensate the man for any animals that might be lost.

Twenty dogs leapt from their crates, eager to please their master.

"Come here, dogs," The trainer held an old T-shirt that the dogs sniffed, soaking the scent. "Good, good."

Without prompting, the dogs started the search, a scrawny healer finding the trail first, letting out a long howl.

"They've got it," announced Everette Turner, the dog trainer.

Max Laney smiled. "Let them run."

———

HOLLIE BANGED on the rickety door. "Eli! You home?" He was getting soaked from the awning that let in more rain than it kept out. His old friend had let the place go to hell.

"Who's there?" came the call from inside.

"It's Hollie. Open the door dammit."

"Hold your horses."

Hollie waited as the plethora of deadbolts unlocked, the door finally opening.

Eli Henderson, bow-legged, hunched and withered, looked like a shell of the man he'd once been. Ten years Hollie's senior, the two men hadn't become acquainted until the 1990's when they'd met a common enemy: Max Laney. Eli and Hollie were two of the last hold-outs to Laney's complete takeover of decent land in Defuniak Springs. Each had the benefit of controlling key pieces in the overall landscape, lots that the greedy Laney wanted badly.

"What are you doing out in the rain?"

Hollie stomped inside, shaking the water from his hair. "Waiting for you to let me in."

Eli looked his friend up and down. "What the hell happened to you?"

"Give me a cup of coffee and I'll tell you."

ELI LISTENED INTENTLY as Hollie recounted the incredible tale. When he was finished, Eli asked, "So where's the kid now?"

"Out there doing what he does best."

"Marine sniper you said?"

Hollie nodded. "A damn good one too. They don't nominate just anyone for the Congressional Medal of Honor."

Eli scratched his stubbly chin. "What do you want me to do?"

"Do you still have that stash in your attic?"

A crooked smile. "Damn right I do. Been meaning to use it too. Come on. Let's go take a look."

———

THE DOGS WERE WELL TRAINED, rarely having to double

back despite the storm. Ten of Laney's men followed, trying to keep up, grumbling as they struggled through the brush. The occasional bark from the scouts led them on through the soaked vegetation, further into the gloom.

———

"YOU WANT to tell me how you got your hands on all this?" Hollie looked around like kid in a candy store.

"I don't know. Just collected it over the years."

"You better hope the police never see this."

"I'll be dead and gone before that happens. Besides, it sounds like we'll get to use it before the day's out."

Hollie had known Eli Henderson was a connoisseur of sorts for military weaponry, but the amount of firepower in the old man's attic reminded him of the armories he'd visited during his time in the Army. "And you sure you're okay with me taking some of it?"

"Shoot, I'm going with you."

"Now, Eli, are you sure you're in good enough condition..."

Eli scowled. "I may look like an old fart, but I can still fire a weapon, better than you I'll bet."

Hollie couldn't argue with him. He needed all the help he could get. A thought came to him suddenly. "Who else do you think might lend us a hand?"

The old man grinned. "I know just the people."

———

"WAS HE THERE?" Max Laney asked the rain-soaked man.

"No, sir. The house and the barn were empty."

"And his truck?"

"Still there."

"Did you do what I told you?"

"Yes, Mr. Laney."

"Good. Now, here's what I want you to do next."

———

SINCE IT WAS CENTRALLY LOCATED, Hollie and Eli decided to use Henderson's home as a staging area. Their recruiting efforts had already drummed up a handful of recruits, all men, all senior citizens. They pulled up in a mix of battered cars, rusted jeeps and polished Hummers. Hollie knew some of them, but they were Eli's men.

The loose band of men had met through the years, some dying off, others moving to the area and taking their place. Most were bachelors, seeking the camaraderie of men with similar values, hard-working men who believed in an honest day's work and helping your neighbor. All were veterans of the military, a smaller number having served in World War II, some in Korea and others in Vietnam.

They spent summer nights together, toasting to friends dead and gone. When one of their number was too feeble to leave home, the others would bring the food and drink, never leaving their sick friend alone. Goodbyes were never said. Their favored farewell a solemn, "See you soon."

They came from all over, but had settled in the Pandhandle, seeking warmer weather and a quiet place to live out their remaining days. They found each other through service clubs, the VA and the VFW. Most importantly, they came when called.

Seven had braved the weather and sat chatting in Eli's cluttered living room.

Hollie and Eli stood to the side. "Are you sure about this?" asked Hollie.

"I trust these men with my life, and you know that's a lot for me to admit."

"Okay. Let's talk to them."

Eli hadn't told his friends a thing, only that he needed their help. He'd thought about what to say, not wanting to mince words. He coughed into his hand silencing the veterans. "First, thanks for coming. You know I wouldn't have asked if it wasn't important." Nods around the room. "Second, some of you know Hollie Herndon. Good man. I'm proud to call him my friend. We won't talk about the fact that he was an Army doggie." More nods, and a couple wry grins. There was more than one former soldier in the group. "Here's the deal, I'm not gonna lie, what we're about to do is damn dangerous. I don't want anyone in it if they don't want to be. Now's your chance. If you want out, feel free to leave. No hard feelings."

He waited. Not a man moved. Good men.

Eli nodded. "Okay, now that we're all in, let's talk business."

CHAPTER THIRTY-SIX

Max Laney's troops were deployed. He hadn't heard from the group with the hounds, but he felt the plan coming together. The rest of his men were in place. It helped that Laney owned or controlled most of the land in the surrounding vicinity. He knew it well.

Still no word from the police, but he was sure that the Marine had gotten Knox as well. It would've been good to have the chief on his side. without him Laney couldn't use the police department, and he didn't dare try. Too many possible complications.

He was on his own to wage the battle on his home turf. Laney was confident in his resources. They'd never failed him before. It had never been a Marine sniper he'd hunted down, but there was always time for a first.

No, Laney trusted his instincts, and they told him that as long as he threw the full weight of his influence into finding and killing Briggs, it would happen.

Max Laney puffed on a pudgy cigar wondering how Gen. Douglas McArthur had felt before sending troops into battle. He'd have to read about it after the war was won.

———

HOLLIE AND ELI divided their men into two teams. Eli would take the less mobile in two trucks, and Hollie would command the rest.

With marching orders in hand, the years melted away from their grizzled appearance. The spark of youth and the bond of brotherhood reignited something in them that could only come in times of need. It was like a platoon getting ready to step off on a patrol, joking to calm the nerves.

Watching the men from a distance, Hollie's memories floated back to his days in the Army, when he'd been a cocky Lieutenant ready for anything. He was far from that now, but being amongst fellow warriors brought a similar feeling of fraternity. He wasn't as reckless as he'd once been, but he had years of experience on his side.

Eli looked up from the conversation he was having with a tiny man with jaundiced features. "You ready, Hollie?"

"Let's go."

Grabbing the weapons they'd been issued from Eli's armory, the men walked out into the strong wind and rain, warriors once again.

———

THEY'D BEEN at it for hours, their energy draining as the last remnants of daylight faded. The dogs had slowed too, eagerly taking the tidbits of food from their master.

"How long do we have to be out here?" asked one of the hired guns, pistol stowed carelessly in his pocket.

"Let me call Mr. Laney and see if the guy turned up," suggested another man. A minute later he shook his head. "He said to keep going. Hey, dog man, how come your bitches haven't found the guy?"

Everette Turner, a sturdy man in his mid-forties, looked around. "Have you seen what we're walking through?" In response the woods shook with a rattle of thunder. "My dogs are good, but this could take a while."

By the look on his face it was obvious that Turner was a patient man and in no hurry. They were the opposite, men of action who'd sooner throw a sucker punch in the back of an unsuspecting man's head than to wait for anything.

"Feels like we've been going in circles," said the first man, wiping his brow with the back of his hand. "How much is Mr. Laney paying you anyways?"

"That's my business. You better stick to yours if you want to get paid." The trainer barked an order to his dogs and they jumped off in pursuit.

Silently, Turner wondered if he should've taken the job. Max Laney had told him that a criminal was on the loose and he'd taken him for his word. Why wouldn't he? Turner wasn't from Defuniak Springs, but he'd heard of the wealthy family. Plus, it had been a slow month and he'd welcomed the chance to make up for it.

After searching the wilderness for hours with men who were obviously thugs, the trainer, a former military police-man, had his doubts about Laney's true purpose. The description of the man they were looking for was vague. The reason even more so.

"A thieving bum," was what Laney had said. "Gave him some work around the house and he stole my equipment from the shed." He'd produced a shirt he said belonged to the thief. Turner now wondered how Laney had it in his possession.

All these thoughts sifted through Turner's mind as he followed the pack, Laney's goons complaining every step of the way.

———

THE FIRES still burned when Hollie pulled up to his property. Both the house and the barn. More than anything, the memories were lost. His wife calling for dinner from the front porch. His young son dangling from the tire swing Hollie had put up on his fifth birthday. All gone. Swept away once, now gone forever.

"You still want to go in?" asked one of his companions.

"No use now. Let's stick to the plan. We have everything we need."

Hollie turned away from the home he'd known since birth, the taste of revenge on his tongue, metallic, harsh, yet enticing.

CHAPTER THIRTY-SEVEN

First one then all of the dogs bayed. Everette Turner sped into a trot, the men behind him perking up and following. The rays from their flashlights led the way, eventually shining on the dogs who had arrayed around a large tree. The trainer followed their gazes, approaching with gun drawn.

"Is it him?" asked one of the mercenaries.

Turner ignored the question, still trying to see into the heavily vegetated tree, rain and darkness making it nearly impossible to see past the first level of branches.

Moving around the behemoth cautiously, Turner spied an opening in the canopy, squinting through the downpour.

"You can point your guns at the ground," he announced to the men who'd constantly maintained poor muzzle awareness, repeatedly pointing their weapons at him.

"What is it?"

"Dead deer. Strung up there." Turner pointed, up to where a doe had been wedged in between branches, entrails hanging, dripping blood to the ground.

"Why in the hell would someone want to do that?"

The trainer moved to his dogs, trying to get them to

move away from the carcass. Even well-trained dogs could go astray at the smell of that much food. It didn't help that they were tired and hungry. It was all he could do to get them to listen and stop their howling.

To make matters worse, one of the Laney's idiots decided to climb up into the tree and try to dislodge the animal. This sent the dogs into a frenzy.

"I think I got..." The man in the tree was cut off with a muffled *THUMP*, followed by the deer falling to the ground. Every dog except the one Turner held by the collar jumped to retrieve the prize.

So enthralled were the men with the scene of the ravenous dogs attacking the carcass on the ground that no one remembered the man in the tree, except Everette Turner. Letting the last dog join the feast, Turner pointed his flashlight into the tree.

"I think one of you better help your friend," he commented nonchalantly.

A ruddy faced hire looked at him questioningly. "What are you talking about?"

Turner simply pointed up. The man's gaze lifted along with his flashlight beam. It took him a moment to make out. "Holy shit."

More beams, more curses. The man in the tree sat with his back to the trunk, legs straddling a large branch, blood running from his mouth from the large stake impaled through his chest.

Bum my ass, thought Turner.

———

TWO BLASTS RATTLED the thick glass, making Max Laney turn from the kitchen table where he'd been monitoring the progress from his teams. The power still wasn't on, but Laney could see where the blast had come from. The double garage that sat detached from the main house lay in a heap, wisps of smoke barely visible.

"What the...?"

One of the men who'd stayed behind to guard the main house ran into the room. "Mr. Laney, two rockets or something from the road. Whoever it was raced off before we could follow."

"Rockets?"

"Yes, sir. That's what it looked like."

What was the purpose? Why not target the house instead? And more importantly, who the hell was helping Hollie? Laney had made sure Herndon's farm was burnt to the ground. Another wrench thrown into this plans.

"Did you see what the car looked like?"

"No, sir. We couldn't see that far. I don't know how they shot the garage from so far away."

The man was right. With the limited visibility surely it would have been impossible to take one shot, let alone two, unless...

The only people he knew that had that type of weaponry, possibly with night vision or infrared capability was the military. Laney wondered if maybe Briggs had called in the Marines, but that was impossible. It had to be someone local, someone with access, or maybe even a stockpile of military-grade weaponry.

Laney searched his mental database, sifting through the all the locals he knew. His breath caught as his brain lingered on one name: Eli Henderson.

———

ELI HENDERSON COULDN'T STOP laughing. "I wish I could

see the look on Max's face. I hope his Lexus was in the garage."

They sped along the flooded roadway, headed to their next task, every man smiling, reliving the days when they would have charged the objective on foot. That wasn't their job this night. They had more important things to take care of.

———

ONCE THE DOGS had satisfied their appetites, Turner was able to corral them and work on finding the trail. As he reached into his pack a prickle ran up his spine. Someone was watching. Turner could feel it even though the dogs didn't notice.

Pivoting slowly, the experienced woodsman faced the opposite direction, away from the rest of the men. Frozen in place, eyes focused into the darkness, Turner swept his right hand from left to right, only visible to someone in the distance. He repeated the motion hoping someone was actually watching and that it wasn't just his nerves playing tricks on him.

CHAPTER THIRTY-EIGHT

Wally looked up at the sound of the front door opening. Business had been slow because of the storm and he was anxious to make any money he could. The place was empty. After the scuffle with the Laneys, he wondered more than once why he stayed.

Hollie stomped his feet on the door mat. "Good evening, Wally."

Wally groaned, his stomach twisting in knots. "Now, I don't want any trouble, Mr. Herndon. I'm just trying..."

The old man held up his good hand. "I'm not here to make trouble, son. I just want to ask you a few questions."

Thinking of the warning he'd gotten from Max Laney, the bar owner hesitated. All he wanted to do was close up, go home, and ride out the storm. "I don't know if I should."

"Worried about Laney?"

"Of course. You saw what he did to my place. Johnny's as crazy as they come, but Mr. Laney will tear my life apart if he wants to."

"Do you owe him money?"

"I do, just like most of us in this town."

"What if I told you that if you help us, you'll be free and clear of Laney's loan?"

Wally scowled, not able to believe the words. He'd been in Laney's debt ever since he'd moved to town. First it was a helping hand. Next it was a small loan to buy the bar. Every time the economy went south, Wally had no choice but to seek assistance from Laney.

"Unless you have a whole lot of money, I don't see how you can say that."

Hollie smiled. "Let's just say Laney's time is about up. Now, are you with us or against us?"

"Who's us?"

"Come on. Let me introduce you."

———

THE HAMMERING HAD STOPPED. Laney walked through the house, inspecting the work, one of the hired hands following close behind. "Did you get the front door?"

"We did, Mr. Laney."

"Good. Have the others get everything cleaned up and then meet me in the kitchen. I want to go over what happens next."

"Uh, Mr. Laney, some of the boys were wondering if we might take turns getting a little shut eye. It's been a long day, and..."

Laney's eyes narrowed. "I'm not paying you to sleep. You tell the others that if I find one of them dozing off, so help me..."

Cowering slightly at the silent rage radiating off of his employer, the man nodded and left to find the others.

———

THEY'D DECIDED to leave the body in the tree instead of trying to drag it along after the dogs. One of the men made a note of the GPS coordinates and plodded on after the others.

Their pace had slowed considerably despite Everette Turner's lead. Time after time he had to stop and wait for the rest of the group to catch up. He wondered how effective they'd be when they caught up to their quarry. Just before continuing from where they'd found the dead deer, Turner had overheard some of the men talking, betting who would deliver the killing blow to the fugitive.

Laney had told Turner the wanted man was to be brought back alive. Either the posse had other expectations or Laney had lied. Turner believed the latter.

On they marched, he following the sounds of his dogs, the rest lost in their misery, bitching with every step.

Minutes later, they demanded another stop. Turner nodded and found a tree to stand under, wondering how long the rest would last. He'd brought enough energy bars and water to last a day. If needed he knew he could make it last for three.

The others hadn't planned as well. The one's who had brought anything to eat brought an assortment of candy and snacks. Most had finished their supply barely an hour into the hunt. Turner could see the strain in their sunken eyes. They were dehydrated and exhausted.

"Where's Pete?" asked one of the men, blowing a cloud of cigarette smoke into the air, his rifle leaning against a tree.

"I think he went to take a leak," came the answer from another.

Five minutes later, still no Pete.

"Pete! Pete!" went the call into the darkness. No reply except for the deluge from above.

"Hey, dog man. Bring your bitches back and help us find Pete," barked the ringleader.

Turner shook his head. "I'm not getting paid to babysit you boys. Mr. Laney's paying me to find one man. Now, I suggest you send a couple of your men to do a quick search for Pete. In five minutes I'm heading off that way."

The leader of the band contemplated Turner's words, the indecision plain on his face. Pushed to the point of exhaustion, the man was having a hard time focusing. "Fine." He shined his flashlight at two others. "You and you. Do a quick loop around, but keep us in sight. Pete probably went to take a dump and fell asleep shittin' on a log."

The joke went over flat and the two lucky picks stomped off in separate directions to look for their missing member.

———

SCOTT CARR, a diminutive man with a pot belly, dirty ball cap drooping, tried to focus on the way he was going, but his head pounded from dehydration. Looking up at the sky he opened his mouth to drink the rain, his own supply having been consumed long ago.

The moment did little to alleviate the headache or his thirst. He sighed and pointed his flashlight at the ground, looking to avoid more falls in the slippery mud. Something moved. He looked closer, wondering if it was a trick of the light on the water. Again the movement.

Carr moved closer, the finger of his right hand tense on the trigger. Suddenly, like a scene from a horror movie, a dark form that looked like an elongated bush, sprang from the mud causing Carr to fumble with his weapon, dropping it to the ground.

Stumbling backwards, a scream stuck in his throat, Carr kept his shaking flashlight focused on the two eyes, glowing like a snake's, as they took him down.

TURNER WATCHED as Laney's men went back and forth, cursing and grumbling as if it would make a difference.

"Where the fuck is, Scotty?"

Lucky pick #2 returned empty handed. They'd waited ten more minutes for Scott Carr.

"I'll bet he went home. Said he was feeling sick," offered one of the men.

"Laney's gonna kill him if he finds out. Scotty! Scotty!" The calls tried to pierce the blackness. Again, no reply.

"Gentlemen, I suggest we keep moving. My dogs are getting jumpy." Turner had recalled his pack that now paced eagerly around their master.

Once more the indecision from the leader. "Shit. Okay, let's get going."

On a clipped command from Turner, his dogs bounded off into the darkness, far less hindered than their human companions. The trainer took one last look at the others and followed his hounds.

CHAPTER THIRTY-NINE

"Everyone ready?" Hollie looked to his men, all except Wally nodding grimly. The bar owner sat in the back of the suburban looking like he might vomit at any moment.

They'd managed to recruit three more men, in addition to Wally. All were in some kind of debt to Max Laney.

Hollie knew that what they were doing was risky, but they didn't have much of a choice. Everything started and ended with Max Laney.

They made it the rest of the way on foot, leaving the vehicle parked on the side of the road. Hollie took a deep breath. His mind made up, he pressed forward, walking far enough inside the tree line that he could still see Laney's driveway. There wasn't a soul in the front yard. While that seemed somewhat odd to the ranger's recollection of a proper perimeter defense, Hollie assumed that Laney had consolidated his resources to the main house.

Hollie signaled a halt, and extracted his night vision scope. He panned from side to side, looking for any sign of movement or light. Nothing from the grounds or the house.

A moment later they were moving, the military veterans

taking the lead. Once they were as close to the house as they were going to get without being in the open, Hollie did one more inspection with his scope. Nothing.

"I'll go in first. If I get to the door, you follow."

Nods from the men.

Keeping his profile as low as his body would allow, Hollie prowled across the drive and up to the house. He could just make out the boarded up windows and front door. Stepping up onto the front porch, Hollie took a knee, listening. Only the steady rain and occasional thunder.

Two men followed, soon kneeling next to Hollie.

"No way in on the front side. Let's head around back."

"You want me to go first, Hollie?" asked Mickey Tomes, a wiry black man who'd been a green beret in Vietnam. He held an M16-A2 ready in his gnarled hands.

"No. You wave the others over, then follow a few feet behind. I don't want any booby traps taking more than one of us out."

Hollie crept his way around the house, slow steady steps. Still no resistance. He could now see the back porch where he and Daniel had talked with Laney. That seemed like weeks before. No sign of anyone, but the back door wasn't boarded shut.

He waited for the others to catch up. Mickey Tomes was the first.

"Anything?"

"The back door isn't boarded up. I'm going to try that first."

"I'll go with you."

Hollie nodded, motioning for the other to stay put.

Seconds later, Hollie and Mickey had their backs to the stone facade, the door between them. Hollie tried to see inside, even using the light sensitive night vision scope. Nothing. No movement. No light.

On a whim, Hollie tried the doorknob, slowly. It turned and the door slid open. Mickey had his weapon trained into the dark interior, his eyes trying to pick up the outline of the enemy. Nothing.

Knowing he was limited by his wounded arm, Hollie signaled for Mickey to go first. With a nod, the old green beret glided in, stepping cautiously on the tile kitchen floor.

"Clear," he whispered as Hollie's eyes adjusted to the deeper dark inside.

His ears felt suddenly sensitive as the muffled rain beat down relentlessly outside, but the house was still. Hollie inspected the area with his scope, the image much clearer than it had been outside. No sounds. No movement.

He poked his head out the back door and motioned for the others to follow. They would search the house with all but two of the men who would guard the exit.

The six men made it to the formal dining room when they heard shots from the back yard. Hollie rushed back to the kitchen. A body lay in the doorway, one of his latest recruits, Earl Newland, a pudgy alcoholic who'd lost his family farm to Max Laney the year before.

Hollie backed away from the door, taking cover behind the granite-topped island. He'd just made it to the far side of the kitchen to see if he could get a better vantage point when a shot cracked in the distance, the round shattering dark granite just above Hollie's head a nanosecond later.

———

"DID YOU GET HIM?"

"Just missed, I think."

Max Laney patted the man on the back. "Keep them pinned down." Extracting a small flashlight from his rain slicker, Laney flashed it twice toward the house.

———

HOLLIE SAW the flashes in the distance, followed by thumping sounds from above. Footsteps on the roof. He thought he heard a vehicle engine.

A moment later, he watched as Earl Newland's body slid out of the doorway. "What the..." The white paneled van scraped its way into place, effectively blocking the exit.

———

LANEY PULLED a small control panel that was encased in a waterproof bag out of his pack. Flipping a toggle switch, the panel lit up green. Looking at his house one last time, Laney clicked all four buttons, imagining the chaos inside his old home.

———

HOLLIE HEARD a pop and then a scream from the adjoining room.

"Fire!"

The first small explosion was followed by three more. The kitchen ceiling glowed red hot and then the flames came, hungrily devouring the wood beams.

The others had converged in the kitchen, looking to Hollie for guidance. He was momentarily at a loss, having just led his troops into an ambush.

CHAPTER FORTY

Men were dropping like flies. After the fourth man disappeared, the search party leader kept everyone in a tight group, warning the others that he wasn't above shooting them if they fled.

Turner watched it all with amusement. The hunters had become the hunted. A small part of the former military policemen wondered if the man in the shadows would differentiate him from the rest of the bunch. He knew it was pointless to worry. He'd learned long ago that whatever was going to happen would happen. Still, he kept his weapon holstered, hoping that the sight of less aggression could help his odds.

His dogs had gotten so far out in front that he'd had to resort to using the rudimentary tracking device he'd picked up from a trade show in the spring. It didn't tell him how far the dogs were, but it did show him which way to go. That along with his GPS and the electric training collars each of the dogs wore, was all that had kept the group on some kind of course.

As he waited for his spotty GPS signal to refresh, he continued moving forward.

———

THE HEAT ASSAULTED the men from every angle. Smoke poured in, making them cough in fits, obscuring their vision. One man tried to break through a barricaded window only to be greeted with a bullet to the face.

They were trapped. Hollie's mind searched for a way out. "To the basement!" he yelled over the crackle of flame, running farther into the house. The door leading to the bottom level was barricaded, but with the help of the others, the thick plywood peeled back.

Streaming through through the opening, the men gulped in the fresh air from below. Hollie led the way down into the darkness.

———

"YOU'RE SURE?" Max Laney watched the fire fight against the pouring rain as he talked on the phone. "Okay. We'll head that way."

The gunman lying next to Laney looked over once he was sure his boss was off the call. "You want me to stay here and make sure they don't get out?"

"No. I want you with me. If Hollie's merry band of senior citizens is still alive, they won't be for long. Round up the others. I'll meet you at the truck."

Laney stood and watched the burning house for a minute longer, unconcerned by the damage. That's what insurance was for. More importantly, in one grand move, he'd eliminated multiple threats.

"Burn in hell, Hollister Herndon. Your buddy Briggs is next."

———

WALLY ALMOST FAINTED when he shone his flashlight into Johnny's morbid face after running into the chair. "Oh my God!"

Mickey Tomes walked over, holding a torn piece of his shirt over the side of his face that had been scorched by one of Laney's incendiary devices. "Whew. Somebody got that boy good. Was it your friend that did that, Hollie?"

"It was." They'd searched every inch of the spacious basement for a way out. No luck. Smoke started to drift down. Hollie could feel the heat coming through the ceiling. It was only a matter of time before it collapsed. "Come on guys, we need to find a way out."

"I gotta say, fellas, I've been in a pickle or two, but this sure takes the cake," said Mickey. "You think we can get out the way we came?"

"I'll bet the whole first floor is gone. Don't know if we'd make it far," said one of the others.

"I don't know about you guys, but I think I'd rather take my chance running through fire than burning to death down here. What do you say, Hollie?"

Hollie felt the heavy weight of responsibility on his shoulders. These men had come to help, willing to die if need be. The old ranger couldn't let that happen.

———

MAX LANEY TOOK one last look at his home. The roof had caved in several places. He knew the frame would go soon.

Putting it out of his mind, he turned and focused on the last piece of the puzzle.

––––––

ANOTHER MAN GONE. Only a handful left. Everette Turner glanced at his GPS. They'd hit a road junction in under an hour. He wondered what the roving shadow would do next.

His answer came a second later when the ground rose up behind him.

––––––

"TURN OFF THE HEADLIGHTS. They should be right around the corner."

The driver did as Laney ordered, slowing to avoid running off the road. They could see maybe a few feet in front of the truck, rain beating down relentlessly from all angles. A flash from the passenger side.

Laney pointed. "There they are."

Turning the truck to the right, they followed the intermittent flashes guiding them down a side road that had been invisible a moment before. The light blinked twice.

"Park it here. We'll walk the rest of the way."

Laney stepped out into the storm. Five men materialized out of the gloom. "We've got a little shelter set up over here, Mr. Laney."

Once they were all huddled under the makeshift tent, Laney outlined the rest of his plan.

––––––

MICKEY VOLUNTEERED to be the first man up the stairs. It would be his job to get as far as he could and attempt to find the best way out. After a thorough dousing from the wet bar sink, each man lined up at the bottom of the stairs, grim-faced, some shaking slightly. They tied portions of wet clothing over their heads for protection. It wouldn't be much, but it might give them a few precious seconds longer.

"Now remember," said Hollie. "We keep moving no matter what."

They all nodded as Mickey took the first steps up.

CHAPTER FORTY-ONE

Everette Turner didn't move. He couldn't. Something had wrapped around him like an anaconda, his mouth covered by what felt like a spongy paw. He didn't resist, not even when he heard muttering from above and the splashes accompanying someone's passing. It wasn't that he was afraid. It had been the quiet, "Shhh," in his ear as he'd been lowered to the soggy earth, the cold steel blade pressed against his throat.

———

"DOG MAN! Yo, dog man, where the fuck are you?!"

The hunting party shone their flashlights in every direction, as if warding off evils spirits. Fewer than half of their original number remained. They'd deluded each other into thinking that those missing had slipped off into the night, deserters to a man.

"Maybe he's too far off to hear us," offered one of the men.

"He was just up ahead of us. I saw him looking at his GPS. Dog man!"

Still no answer.

The leader of the ragged band looked down at his GPS. "There's a road not far up ahead. Maybe he's up there."

The prospect of a real road to walk on instead of the ankle sucking mud of the wild perked the men up. Now in a single file line, they moved off.

———

THE PRESSURE EASED off of Turner's mouth, then off of the rest of his body. Easing his way around, coming to one knee, he tried to make out what he was looking at.

Whatever it was looked like the outline of Bigfoot, hairy and oversized. It took a second for him to realize what it was, a ghillie suit.

"Who are you?" Turner whispered.

"Go home," answered the camouflaged man in a raspy voice, turning away, already fading into the night.

A chill flittered down Turner's back. He'd met killers before. He'd hunted them for years in some of the worst parts of the world. Something about the way this man moved, the expression in his eyes, disconnected...

Standing in the pouring rain, Turner shivered, only remembering a minute later to depress the button that would electronically recall his dogs. One silent thanks and he walked back the way they'd come.

———

MICKEY BURST through the flaming door at the top of the stairwell, ending up on the ground. The wave of heat assaulted the next man in line, stopping their movement cold.

"Keep moving!" yelled Hollie.

Three more steps in, Mickey back on his feet, another man collapsed. It was Wally. Hollie bent to help him up.

"I'll get him," coughed Mickey. "You find a way out."

Hollie looked all around, but all he could see was orange and grey, walls of flame and smoke laughing at the old men in their wake with their crackles and spit.

Chunks of wood and drywall fell from an opening overhead.

Suddenly a deafening crash caused Hollie to crouch, hands covering his head, waiting for the fatal blow to fall.

———

THE BARKING WAS ALL the warning they had. Appearing like swifts ghosts out of the nightfall, the dogs ignored the hunting party, running the opposite way that the men were slogging.

"What the hell?"

One of the men tried to catch a passing hound, only to be snapped at by three of its companions. They were gone in a flash, howling at some unseen quarry.

"Where the fuck do you think they're going?"

"Who gives a shit. Let's get to the road. I'm tired and hungry."

Soaked and exhausted, not one of the men thought differently. With the road so close, they trudged on, not thinking twice about the retreating bloodhounds.

———

"DID YOU HEAR THAT?"

Max Laney nodded. "That was Turner's dogs. They should

be here soon. Everyone keep a lookout, weapons at the ready."

His men had taken shelter where they could, rifles and shotguns pointing across the road. Laney smiled, gripping a last surprise in his hand. It would be over soon.

———

WATER SPRAYED on Hollie as strong hands gripped him under the armpits, dragging him forward. He couldn't see. The heat continued to assault his senses, his consciousness waning.

Then suddenly, he was clear of the burning house, rushed down the front steps and dumped unceremoniously in the muddy front yard. He looked up, his vision clearing slightly, taking in the yellow grin of the man hunched over him.

"Did you think we'd leave all the fun to you?" said Eli Henderson.

———

MAX LANEY WATCHED the road through infrared goggles, a present from his late wife. The dogs hadn't appeared, but he could see a white blur moving closer. He assumed it was his men. Soon he could make out five forms moving and lifted the goggles. There were using their flashlights.

"Idiots," murmured Laney. But it didn't matter. He hadn't really expected them to capture or even find the elusive Marine sniper. They were part of his plan, but in a different way. They were the bait.

He repositioned his goggles and waited.

———

HOLLIE FINISHED GULPING the bottle of water that Eli had given him. "Did you see where Max went?"

Eli nodded. "We saw two trucks take off up Highway Eighty Three. Pretty sure one of them was Laney's."

"Let's head that way. There's a lot of road, but maybe we'll get lucky."

———

THE REMAINING MEMBERS of the search party breathed a collective sigh of relief at the feel of asphalt under their feet.

"Our guys should be right across the road. Come on."

They followed the man with the GPS, not one sensing the presence closing in from behind.

———

LANEY WATCHED the men cross the road, dismayed, but not surprised, by the small number. His heartbeat thudded faster when he caught a spot of white in the distance, moving. It was faint, but it was there.

Settling his breathing as he would on a safari hunt, Max Laney counted down the seconds, measuring the distance, his hand squeezing a bit harder.

———

JUST AS THE weary group reached the opposite side of the pavement, a thunderous explosion rocked the area, sending the men to the ground. A second later, the rest of Laney's men assaulted on line across the road, firing as they moved.

———

LANEY HAD DETONATED the three claymores he'd personally emplaced in the kill zone. The hunting party had done their part, leading the sniper right into the ambush. Rising from his hidden position, Laney only hoped that Daniel Briggs wasn't dead yet. He wanted to be the one to put a bullet in his head. He'd promised his men a bonus to whoever brought him back alive, even if he was just barely alive.

CHAPTER FORTY-TWO

Hollie looked out the window. "Jesus. Was that thunder?"

"Sounded like an explosion to me," said Eli, not taking his eyes off the waterlogged road.

Hollie's stomach tightened. "It came from up ahead."

"I'm going as fast as I can. Any faster and we'll be off the road."

"Do what you can, Eli. I'm afraid we might be too late."

———

I HEARD FIRING. The repeated shots from a high caliber rifle. Booms from a shotgun, or was it two? Was I dreaming?

Opening my eyes to the pelting rain. No pain. That was good. I tried to sit up. I couldn't. Something was on top of me, but not uncomfortably so. Feeling with my fingers, rough, slick, a tree trunk. But how?

My mind searched for the answer. The animal that had taken over my body tried to force its way back into control. I couldn't let it. Resisting the temptation of slipping back into my primal state, I strained to get free of the fallen tree, and the firing moved closer.

———

MAX LANEY WATCHED his men move, hoping they would find Briggs alive. If they didn't and he was dead, it wouldn't matter. The firing slowed as the men stalked cautiously, calling to one another as they closed in.

———

"WHAT'S THAT UP AHEAD?" Hollie squinted into the distance.

"I think it's a light. Should I slow down?"

"No. Keep going."

It looked like someone was trying to flag them down. The rain had subsided just enough. They barreled down the pavement, Hollie's eyes narrowing.

"Go faster."

"But..."

"Just do it."

Eli pressed the pedal nearly to the floor, still worried about the standing water that could send them careening out of control at any moment. He gripped the wheel and focused forward. His hooded eyes went wide as he realized there was a person standing in the middle of the road.

Hollie saw his friend pull off the gas. His voice came out like the rasp of a reaper, "Run him over."

Eli hesitated, but Hollie grabbed the old man's knobby knee and pressed it down, revving the engine, RPMs jumping.

They both saw the shock on the man's face right before they slammed into him, the danger registering too late, the flashlight and shotgun flew high, the crumpled body trampled by the speeding truck.

———

LANEY TURNED to the left seeing headlights in the distance. They'd posted a man in each direction to redirect drivers. Obviously the idiot they'd put on the south end of the road hadn't listened. Laney cursed and rose to meet the vehicle.

———

THE TRUCK'S high beams cut into the night, aided by the miraculous respite of rain. Hollie saw them first. A line of men moving into the tree line. Putting his submachine gun to his shoulder, his companions in the cab doing the same, he opened fire, rounds smashing though the windshield.

———

LANEY'S MEN were temporarily blinded by the blast of the headlights, half turning away, the others ripping the night vision goggles from their faces. The first man went down in a hail of bullets that reached out and touched the man next to him, sending them both to the ground.

The two marauding vehicles tore into Laney's ranks, old men now young again, disciplined, ruthless, deadly, avenging angels.

———

JAW CLENCHED, Max Laney backed away from his position, watching as the roughnecks went down all too quickly. The remaining group of hunters had come to the road, curiously, stupidly, only to be mowed down, looks of shock plastered to their faces.

Cursing his string of bad luck, Laney hopped into the truck and took off in the opposite direction.

———

ELI HENDERSON SEARCHED THE BODIES, all dead save one, and he would die shortly. "I'd say we did pretty good, boys. Just like the old days."

His comrades joined the search, grimly going to task, adrenaline still coursing like a raging drug, keeping them young if only for a few more minutes. More than one man knelt down to say a silent prayer over the dead, not because of regret, but because above all, these warriors knew the worth of life. They'd fought and bled for their country in lands far from its shores. They'd left as boys and come back men. They'd lost friends, some family.

Hollie was the most frantic, searching each man methodically, hoping Daniel was not among them. "Daniel! Daniel!"

Soon the others repeated the call, spreading the line, moving into the woods.

———

I HEARD THE CALLS. They sounded like muted gurgles. Maybe it was a trick. They couldn't blow me up or shoot me. Maybe Laney was trying something new.

I felt rather than heard them moving closer, my mind realizing my hearing had dulled from the explosion. Squirming under the push of the tree, I stopped. Something about one of the voices pierced the ringing in my ears.

Hollie?

———

HOLLIE HEARD IT FIRST, thinking it another survivor from Laney's cadre, he moved in cautiously.

A grated sound, like a man gasping his last breath. Closer. Closer.

"Hayi. Hayee. Haay," came the voice.

Hollie panned his flashlight back and forth, zeroing in on the sound. Most of the vegetation was shorn, a result of the claymores. A large tree lay up ahead. Movement. A hand waving.

CHAPTER FORTY-THREE

The men stared at me as I gulped down my fourth bottle of water. To say that I was parched was an understatement. I don't think they knew what to make of me. I probably looked like a monster with my makeshift camouflage, most of which I didn't remember putting together. The beast had done it without my help.

They'd managed to pull me out from under the giant log unscathed. Despite my reassurance that I wasn't hurt, one of the men, a former Navy corpsman, inspected me from top to bottom.

"Might be a bit dehydrated," said the corpsman, "but other than that, he looks pretty good."

He patted me on the back and joined the working party who were loading bodies into the back of trucks, Hollie among them.

After two protein bars and another bottle of water, I walked over to where Hollie was talking to an ancient looking man, hunched at the waist. They looked up from their conversation.

"Feel better, son?" asked the older gentleman.

"Yes, sir. Thank you for..."

He waved the thanks away. "Us old dogs haven't had this much fun in ages. You'll see when you get to be my age. Times like these...well, let's just say you won't forget them."

I realized that these old men, none younger than sixty, didn't feel a bit of remorse for what they'd done. It was no small thing, waging war in an American town. Brave men.

Hollie interrupted my thoughts. "We'd better get moving soon. Now that the storm's passed there will be people coming down the road."

"What about Laney? Was he with these guys?" I pointed to the stacked cadavers.

"Nope. Not even sure he was here." He turned to the other man. "Eli, let's head back to your place. I'm sure Daniel wouldn't mind getting cleaned up."

As we piled in their vehicles I looked east just as the golden rays of morning cut through the filtering clouds. The beast inside of me howled.

————

MAX LANEY PARKED the SUV in front of his friend's condo. The drive had given him a chance to regroup. He was far from finished, but he needed time.

He'd driven by his beautiful home, now a smoldering ruin. There would be questions from the authorities, but he, Max Laney, could deal with it.

What he needed now was a vacation. Some time to think. Minutes later he climbed aboard his boat, taking in deep breaths of the clear air, savoring the promise of a new day.

Soon he was cruising out of the channel and into the gulf.

————

ELI'S MEN listened with rapt attention to my story. It felt like a dream as I retold my swim to shore in the raging storm. Stealing a running car to get back to Defuniak Springs.

No one batted an eye when I explained how I'd ambushed the police chief or Laney's man, Renley Watts. "Good riddance," said one of the old-timers, spitting on the ground.

"What about the lawyer?" asked Hollie. "It's hard to believe Henry Ellison knew what Laney was up to. He was shocked to see how bad I looked."

I didn't tell them that there had been a moment when anyone I could get my hands on, who had any connection with Max Laney, would die. But in that instant, the beast relented allowing a tiny sliver of my humanity to peak out.

"I put him somewhere safe. Thought he might be useful if we came through it alive."

Hollie nodded with a smile. "That's good to hear. Now, what do we do about Max?"

The beast in me growled. I cut it off with a click of my teeth, grinning wickedly. "Don't worry about Max. He's mine."

———

DEFUNIAK SPRINGS WAS COMING BACK to life, crews working hard to clear roadways and restore power as quickly and efficiently as possible. The citizens knew natural disaster well, and most had weathered their fair share of tropical storms and hurricanes. Neighbor helped neighbor.

So it was with Eli's band of warriors. Dispersed in separate directions, we soon had a plan concocted, one that would not only cover our tracks, but would see the Laney empire dismantled piece by piece.

———

HENRY ELLISON SHADED his eyes from the sun when we opened the woodshed door. I'd tied him to a work bench knowing he was too frail to put up much of a fight.

"Please don't hurt me."

Hollie stepped forward. "Mr. Ellison, it's Hollie Herndon. We have some things to tell you."

———

MAX COULDN'T BELIEVE how calm the gulf was. Once a battle of waves and tides, the emerald water now glass-like, lazily lapping against the vessel's hull. Laney sipped a water glass full of bourbon, savoring the burn running down his throat.

He wasn't in any rush, already having made arrangements for his return home. The course set, Laney enjoyed the soft breeze blowing in through the windows, beckoning him westward.

———

HENRY ELLISON SAT in a state of shock. More than once he'd gasped at Hollie's retelling. I could only imagine what was going through his head. He'd served the Laney family for years, never once questioning their motives. Finding out that he'd been, for intents and purposes, a willing participant in countless schemes of bribery, coercion and outright thievery, I was almost surprised the poor guy didn't keel over and die.

"Are you sure about this, Hollie? I mean, are you really sure?" Ellison's eyes pleaded.

"I'm afraid so, Mr. Ellison. Just sorry you had to hear about it like this."

Ellison nodded, lost in his own thoughts, visibly calculating his next move. To my astonishment, the old man looked up, his eyes burning with determination. "You know, there was a time when a lawyer was afraid to look across the aisle and see Henry Ellison." He stood. "I think it's time to be that man again. Tell me, Mr. Briggs, what can I do to help?"

CHAPTER FORTY-FOUR

He made a stop in Gulfport, Mississippi to buy supplies and a fresh wardrobe. Johnny and Watts had dumped most of the things in the stateroom, and Max Laney would not be seen wearing day-old trousers.

Now freshly showered, wearing a pair of loose khaki shorts and a Tommy Bahama button down shirt, Laney sipped his first cocktail of the night, gazing out at the setting sun from Smuggler's Cove.

There wasn't anything on the tiny Cat Island, but it was close enough to shore that he could stop in at any time. Besides, he'd picked the spot at random, liking the ring of the name Smuggler's Cove, thinking that he'd probably had ancestors who had used the very same spot to smuggle goods into the country.

He lounged on the aft deck, the boat's position giving him a perfect view of the sunset. The only sound that tingled his senses were the occasional screeches from soaring seagulls, doing a pass to see if he had any food.

The sun dipped below the horizon, casting a tangerine glow. Max closed his eyes, lulled by the gently rocking vessel.

———

HE HADN'T BEEN hard to track. I'd gotten lucky. When I ambushed Renley Watts, I found the GPS locator he'd used to track me and Hollie before. It even had a piece of blue tape with *Herndon* stuck above one of the small screens. Next to it was another name, on the same blue painter's tape. It said *Laney's Boat*.

———

THE GLASS almost slipped from his hand, but he grasped it before it fell. *Must have dozed off*, thought Laney, shaking his head. Yawning, he lifted the nearly empty glass to his mouth when a searing pain tore through his leg. He screamed in shock, almost falling out of his seat when he tried to stand and look down.

The pain was unbearable. Laney flipped a switch next to the table and the area was suddenly bathed in soft light. He lifted his throbbing leg and found an arrow, or was is a spear, sticking out of his calf.

"What the…"

A whistle behind him made him turn, the fright clear in his bulging eyes.

"Hello, Max."

———

HE FELT the venom in my voice and backed away a step.

"Briggs?"

I nodded.

Laney looked around, probably looking for something, anything, to use as a weapon. Too bad for him, nothing would help.

"Uh, I'm sure we can talk this through, Mr. Briggs. I'm a wealthy..."

"I don't care about your money." I laughed. "Some other people do though. I'd say right about now your bank accounts are being emptied and the grateful citizens of Defuniak Springs are getting a call from Henry Ellison telling them you've given them their land back."

"What?! I...Henry Ellison is dead." It came out as more of a question. He didn't know. I almost felt sorry for him. Almost. I wanted to let the beast loose, tear him to shreds and sink his body to the ocean floor.

But I couldn't. There was something I had to take care of. "Okay, Max. If you want to keep your money, all you need to do is sign this one piece of paper." I held up a sheet encased in a waterproof bag. "What do you say?"

He scrunched his tanned face, trying to figure out if I was bluffing, not that he had a choice. "Can I see what I'm signing?"

"Sure." I stepped closer, coming within feet of the coward.

"Can I hold it?"

"Nope. You can read it from there."

He looked like he was going to protest, but decided against it, instead reading the document in my outstretched hand. A minute later, his eyes met mine. "This is a power of attorney."

"You're a smart man, Max. Now let's get to signing."

"How do I know you won't go back on your word?"

I smiled. "You don't. You'll just have to trust me."

It took him a moment. "Okay. Let me just go an grab a pen." He started to turn.

"That's okay. I've got one right here." I pulled another waterproof bag out of my waistband, seawater dripping onto the carpet.

Throwing me a hateful look, Laney grabbed the pen. "Can

I at least sit down?" I could see he was trying not to show weakness. I'll bet that fishing spear hurt.

"Sure." I waved him into a white lounge chair and extracted the power of attorney. Standing almost on top of him, I watched as he scrawled his signature on the document. Lifting the paper from the table, I inspected his work. Henry Ellison had shown me a sample of Laney's official signature, just in case he tried to pull a fast one. He hadn't. It matched the one I had seen. I placed the sheet back in its waterproof container.

"Now what? Are you going to let me go?" asked Laney, spitting out every word.

"Tell you what. Why don't you grab each of us a drink," I pointed to the well-stocked bar, "and then we'll cruise back in a few minutes."

Laney nodded, wincing as he got up to prepare the drinks. I turned as well, stowing the pen and paper, re-zipping my wetsuit. "I'll be right back. Gonna take a leak. Don't go below. I'll still be able to see you."

He didn't even turn, knowing he couldn't move fast enough with the spear stuck in his leg.

I walked to the back landing and took my time. My piss splashed into the salt water. Finished, I walked back slowly. Laney had turned his back to me. He'd already downed half of his drink.

I didn't hesitate. In one swift move, I looped the line around his neck two times before he could get his hands up. Yanking Laney to his feet, I turned him around to face me. His eyes wide with fear, blood rushing, he tried to gasp. I was done playing.

"This is for Kelly Waters."

My soul slipped away, replaced in an instant by the creature inside. I watched it like a movie, an innocent bystander, the moves of a monster no more than a tale of horror on my mind's television screen.

Up and over the beast's shoulder went Laney, mouth trying to scream as he flew past the railing, hitting the side of the hull with a loud thud. Wordlessly, mindlessly, the beast tied off the line and walked aft, the sounds of Laney's struggling still thumping against the boat. A moment later the beast was back, a mask of fury as it tied the other end of the line to the fifty pound drifting anchor he'd pulled from the shallow bottom.

I watched silently as my other self untied the line and threw the anchor into the water, taking the still flailing Laney with it to the ocean floor.

The splash quickened my body and I felt my body once again move to my command. I waited. I counted. Three minutes and twenty two second later, the line and Laney's body bobbed to the surface, facedown. I waited another five minutes, watching the body float around the small point of Cat Island.

CHAPTER FORTY-FIVE

We sat in a small coffee shop watching the steady stream of tourists heading in and out on Highway 90.

"You sure you can't stay?" asked Hollie, for the third time.

"I need to keep moving."

"I sure could use your help on the farm. Me and some of Eli's friends would be happy to pay you."

I smiled. "That's a really nice offer, and please tell the others I'm grateful, but my heart tells me there's somewhere else I need to be."

Hollie nodded, looking down at his coffee. "Daniel, I...I know men like you and me, soldiers and Marines who have seen and done things...I know it's hard, son. I sure wish you would let me, or let someone else help you. Lord knows I needed it."

He was right, but I wasn't ready. My demons wouldn't allow it. "I promise I'll try, but I can't do that here."

Hollie reached over and put his hand on mine. "Now listen, if you need anything, anything at all, you make sure you call me. I'll hop on a plane, ride on a train, whatever. You're family now, Marine. I hope you know that."

I patted his hand, genuinely grateful for the old man's words. In another life I might have stopped. I could have stayed. But my mind was set. Something called. I wasn't sure what it was. It didn't matter. I had to go.

"I better get going. My bus will be boarding soon."

We both stood, Hollie looking at me like he wanted to say something else, somehow make me stay. He stuck out his hand.

"It's been an honor meeting you, Marine."

I clasped his hand tight. "The honor was all mine. Semper Fi."

Releasing his grip, I grabbed my pack and headed for the door, resisting the urge to look back as I stepped out into the blazing sun.

―――

I GOT a seat at the back of the bus, next to the window. There weren't many people onboard and I'd figured out how to keep others from sitting next to me.

With a sigh, I opened up my rucksack and pulled out the bottle of Jack Daniels. Twisting the top and breaking the seal, I put the bottle to my lips, once again headed to nowhere.

―――

I hope you enjoyed this story.
If you did, please take a moment to write a review ON AMAZON. Even the short ones help!

GET A FREE COPY OF THE CORPS JUSTICE

**PREQUEL SHORT STORY, *GOD-SPEED*, JUST
FOR SUBSCRIBING AT <u>CG-COOPER.COM</u>**

ALSO BY C. G. COOPER

ABOUT THE AUTHOR

C. G. Cooper is the USA TODAY and AMAZON BESTSELLING author of the CORPS JUSTICE novels (including spinoffs), The Chronicles of Benjamin Dragon and the Patriot Protocol series.

Cooper grew up in a Navy family and traveled from one Naval base to another as he fed his love of books and a fledgling desire to write.

Upon graduating from the University of Virginia with a degree in Foreign Affairs, Cooper was commissioned in the

United States Marine Corps and went on to serve six years as an infantry officer. C. G. Cooper's final Marine duty station was in Nashville, Tennessee, where he fell in love with the laid-back lifestyle of Music City.

His first published novel, BACK TO WAR, came out of a need to link back to his time in the Marine Corps. That novel, written as a side project, spawned many follow-on novels, several exciting spinoffs, and catapulted Cooper's career.

Cooper lives just south of Nashville with his wife, three children, and their German shorthaired pointer, Liberty, who's become a popular character in the Corps Justice novels.

When he's not writing or hosting his podcast, Books In 30, Cooper spends time with his family, does his best to improve his golf handicap, and loves to shed light on the ongoing fight of everyday heroes.

Cooper loves hearing from readers and responds to every email personally.

To connect with C. G. Cooper visit
www.cg-cooper.com